Uncertain Kin

JANICE LYNN MATHER

ANCHOR CANADA

Anchor Canada paperback published 2023
Doubleday Canada hardcover published 2022

LIBRARY AND ARCHIVES CANADA CATALOGUING IN PUBLICATION
Title: Uncertain kin / Janice Lynn Mather.
Names: Mather, Janice Lynn, author.
Identifiers: Canadiana 2022049519X | ISBN 9780385687843 (softcover)
Subjects: LCGFT: Short stories.
Classification: LCC PS8626.A823 U53 2023 | DDC C813/.6—dc23

Cover image: Ghislain & Marie David de Lossy / Getty Images

Printed in the United States of America

Published in Canada by Anchor Canada,
a division of Penguin Random House Canada Limited,
a Penguin Random House company

www.penguinrandomhouse.ca

10 9 8 7 6 5 4 3 2 1

Penguin
Random House
ANCHOR CANADA

For Jason, my chosen
For Nyssa, my soul
For Kayari, my heart

CONTENTS

OTHER PEOPLE'S CHILDREN

CENTIPEDE

"WHO HERE LIKES CENTIPEDES?" the storyteller
began, and like that she spilled warmth all through the
assembly hall, a stuffy barn with six slatted tin shutters
that restricted sunlight. Just that question sparked the
children into a frenzy of titters and squeaks of disgust
and glee at the thought of foot-long beasts with venom-
ous pincers, squirming like snakes and racing like rats,
a near-sea of spider legs propelling their bodies at the
speed, it seemed, of light. Samantha stayed on the outside of this heat. She sat hunched over, arms crossed over
her chest, rubbing her hands from shoulder to elbow and
back up again, to get warm.

"Today," Headmistress Pyfrom had said, minutes earlier,
"we have a special guest, Miss Ramsey, the Story Lady, from

the Ministry of Culture." Miss Ramsey lived two doors down from Samantha. She looked different out of her thin yellow housecoat and red head scarf. Today, she wore a long, sky-blue skirt that lapped at the ground. Samantha shifted in her spot on the floor, then caught her teacher's eye and accompanying stern frown, and sat still, waiting.

"Good morning, boys and girls," the storyteller had said, taking her position at the front of the room. Every class sat on the floor, neatly arranged in rows, grade ones at the front, grade sixes at the rear, each child in their proper place. Unsure whether the usual rules applied to this guest, the students remained quiet. "I said, *Good morning, boys and girls!*"

"Good morning, Mrs. . . ." Here the voices trailed off. A few children—the older, the keeners, those who knew the storyteller from church or the cultural centre, her niece Marie, stashed at the far corner of class 4-P—began carrying "Ram-sey" out, then fizzled at finding their voices nearly alone. Miss Ramsey was untouched. Her smile was wide, she had no cutlass in her hand, yet the sight of her brought coldness to Samantha. An old sensation, like discovering a chewed-up toy in a far corner of a closet, nestled next to an abandoned cockroach husk.

"My name is Mamma Ramsey, the Story Lady." The woman nodded, her round face earnest. Silence met her. "I'm here to tell you an old, old story from before you were born, or before I was born, or—"

"Before Mrs. Pyfrom was born?" Joseph piped up from Samantha's row. Snickers broke out around the hall like a rash.

"Joey!" Mrs. Thompson's voice hissed from the edge of the room. She sat with the other teachers in chairs lined up against the wall, as though they were trying to escape something at the core of this glut of children. Mrs. Thompson shook her head at Joey, *no*. At the front, the headmistress pressed her lips together in a tight smile.

"Yes," Mamma Ramsey, the Story Lady, said, unfazed. "Before even the oldest teacher was born. Older even than the oldest teacher's great-great-grandmother. You all want to hear this story?"

"Yes," a few voices replied. Headmistress Pyfrom tilted her head slightly, her eyebrows lifting expectantly. "Yes, Mamma Ramsey—Miss Ramsey—the Story Lady," the voices added.

And so the storyteller began, *Who here likes centipedes?* Then, in a half-lullaby, half-chanting rhyme: *Once upon a time, was an old, old time, monkey chew tobacco and he spit white lime. Bullfrog jump from bank to bank, while mosquito keep the time. Wasn't my time, wasn't your time. It was old, old time.* Samantha tried to listen to Miss Ramsey be Mamma Ramsey, the Story Lady, but her ears buzzed and whirred and hummed, a steady noise like the washer in the kitchen, the washer that had been broken and that was now fixed. And the more she tried to listen to Mamma Ramsey talking about the centipede, the stronger, louder, heavier that sound became. The woman's lips moved quickly, a charge in the air as the students laughed and fell quiet, in turns. Samantha shut her eyes.

"The centipede was the king of this world. He was short and he was fat, and he had two arms, and he also had only two legs, like you and me. Now, the centipede was very strong, the strongest king in this world . . ."

Pieces of Mamma Ramsey's tale wormed and writhed their way into Samantha's ears, and as they did, she rubbed her arms faster, faster. Her mind whirred through images, spinning until she felt her head must be shaking. Her sister's eyes emptying away. The thin, sweaty man with his under-earth breath, yellowed eyes. Miss Ramsey yelling in her yard, arm raised, then falling, cutlass hacking at some thing in the grass while she yelled, "Centipee! Centipee! Centipee!"

Mamma Ramsey had a particular way of telling stories: leaning forward so her face almost touched those in the front row, feet turned out, scuttling, crablike, when she spoke of underwater things, letting the words lift her up on her tiptoes to become the tiger and the lion, mouth stretched in a vicious snarl. The children watched, wide-eyed. They knew when to pull in their breath in surprise, when to giggle, when to jump.

"And the centipede, at last, was granted his wish. He got ninety-eight new legs," she said. "But he was so tall that he could no longer live in his fancy palace. His wife was now far too tiny to reach up and kiss him, and no one, not even the parrot, could fly up high enough to measure his head for a hat to shade him from the sun. And because he was so tall, he was so much closer to the sun, and he began to pop and sizzle and fry, and that made him madder still. And in despair, the greedy, selfish, mean, grabalicious centipede flung himself down into the cool dirt, and began to writhe in anger, and he still writhes down there today. And sometimes, when it rains heavily, or when someone in the house is greedy or selfish or mean or grabalicious, the centipede comes slithering," here she leaned forward, wriggling her fingers and thumbs like ten of the centipede's offending limbs, "to give a nasty bite as a warning to you to learn from his ways. *Wire bend, story end.*"

There were a few soft, shifting sounds before Mrs. Pyfrom started off the applause. Samantha continued rubbing, rubbing her hands on her arms, the muffled clapping closing in then pulling away, then closing in around her again, like waves.

"What do we say, boys and girls?" Mrs. Pyfrom gazed out over the small bodies, near-identical in their matching shirts and shorts and dresses.

"Thank you, Mrs. Mamma Lady Ramsey the Story Mrs. Lady."

One by one, youngest first, the classes filed out and to their rooms. Samantha kept her head down as her class left, trying to avoid Miss Ramsey.

"Auntie!" Marie hissed, just before Samantha in line, and Miss Ramsey waved and called, "Tell your mummy I ga call her tonight. Keep up with your class, now, alright?" so loudly that Samantha couldn't help but look up, and her eyes and Miss Ramsey's met. Miss Ramsey's face didn't register any emotion, and she turned away, smiling slightly, to speak again with Headmistress Pyfrom. Samantha understood that, as the Story Lady, Miss Ramsey had not wanted to see her, had wanted to pretend that neither of them knew the truth about the centipede.

∞

Mrs. Thompson ordered the children to take out their English exercise books. A rumpling, a rustling, chair legs scraping against tile, pencils rolling across the floor. While the classroom unfolded around her, Samantha clasped the edges of her book. It was a new one, the crisp pages never written in before.

"You need another new book?" Her mother frowned. "Didn't I just give you money for one couple weeks ago? What, you lost it?"

Samantha shrugged.

"Look, I can't keep buying buying buying, you understand? You forget we have to fix the washer, eh?"

Samantha had not forgotten, but said nothing, only waited, until her mother sighed.

"You better be writing or drawing or something in this book, and not eating the paper for a snack," she said, at last. Samantha saw her mother produce a small smile, then hide it, as she fished another seventy-five cents from her change purse. Then her mother snapped it closed with a finality that suggested this would be the last time.

Samantha looked around her. The other children were settling in. Books opened, heads bent over them. Someone sharpened a pencil over the garbage at the front of the class. She peered over at Aaron's book. Aaron crooked a protective arm over his paper, glaring at her. His arm formed a sharp V, the point jutting toward Samantha. Without thinking, she stood up.

"Samantha?" Mrs. Thompson's eyebrows raised, peaks of disapproval. "May I help you?"

Samantha froze.

"Are you going to the dictionary?"

Samantha had no other excuse. She nodded. Mrs. Thompson turned to the blackboard.

The dictionary sat on a table that ran the length of the classroom. In an unsupervised moment, Joey had regaled the class with the definitions of *penis* and *bitch* before the next-door teacher had peeked in to see why class 4-P was suddenly so merry about being left to work for five minutes on their four times tables. Now, Samantha rustled the pages, taking reassurance from their monotony, each page populated by three columns, each entry bolded, each definition spread out in fine font, predictable, orderly.

She flipped through *L*. Lacerate. Lagoon. Leopard. Lie. Noun: A false statement, that which is not true. Verb: To make such a statement. Verb: To rest with. To engage in sexual relations with.

She sat on the broken-down washing machine, staring out the window. She could see clean across to Miss Ramsey's house. Miss Ramsey was clearing her yard. Across the street from Miss Ramsey, the neighbour's boy poked around under the hood of his car. Down the road came a man, bag slung over his shoulder. Even from far away, he didn't look like anyone Samantha knew from their neighbourhood. She turned the other way again, watching Miss Ramsey attack the tall grass against her fence, cutlass clinking against the metal. She leaned against the machine, felt its metallic chill against the backs of her legs.

"Where your sister?" Her grandmother appeared suddenly, marching into the kitchen, reaching around Samantha, snapping the curtains shut. When Samantha said Debbie was in her room, lying down, Grammy turned away, her mouth held as though it was full of bitter leaves. "Get off that machine."

Samantha protested. The machine was the only cool place in the house, and it was broken anyway, hadn't worked for a month.

The knock at the back door was swift, brisk, a chain of taps so close they sounded almost joined together.

"Get. Go outside. Don't come in till I call you," Grammy

snapped at her. "And if your mother come home early, knock. You understand?" Grammy opened the door.

A man stood on the doorstep. He was thin, a deep reddish-brown, skin sweat-smooth. The man who had been slinking down the road. His eyes slid over Samantha, gaze clingy and cold, bristling every hair on her arm. She opened her mouth, then closed it.

"Come to fix the washing machine." He smiled, but so quick it was gone before it had reached his eyes. Samantha climbed off the machine and slipped through the space between the door and this man. She felt his eyes follow her.

Samantha slammed the dictionary shut, sending a draft up her arms.

"Work quietly," Mrs. Thompson advised the class. "Samantha, find your desk."

She sat. She looked over at Aaron's book again, and was rewarded with a kick to the underside of her chair.

"What you lookin' at me for, dummy?" he snapped. Samantha faced forward. Mrs. Thompson had written three questions on the blackboard.

1. Who was the centipede in Mamma Ramsey's story?
2. What happened to the centipede in Mamma Ramsey's story?
3. Write your own folk tale. Be sure that it has a moral, a special lesson about right and wrong.

The questions made no sense. The centipede was the centipede. Who else could a centipede be? Nobody. Nobody. Yet, all around her, children wrote in silence, heads bent over their pages. Aaron bit his lower lip, scowling with concentration. Samantha opened her book.

Outside, she slid from the door to the window, ducked down, listening. Why did she have to be out here and Debbie got to stay inside? She heard Grammy call Debbie, once, twice. Then, a second set of curtains drawn, swishquick. What were they hiding from her inside? The curtains always stayed open in the day. Samantha stood up, strained to see in, but the drapes were pulled tight. She hunched down again. It wasn't fair. One minute. Debbie's voice, No! No! *angry and loud. Grammy's words came to her muffled. Two minutes. Nothing—how could a repairman fix anything and still be so quiet? Samantha reached for the doorknob. Her fingers closed around the smooth surface. She twisted the knob, pushed the door open again.*

The kitchen was a smothered dark, daylight pushing against the drapes. It was empty, the washer as she had left it. She tiptoed in, peered into the dining room.

There, Debbie, standing against the far wall, facing her. Button-up shirt torn open. The man opposite Debbie, his back to the doorway. Debbie stared straight ahead. She should have been looking at the man, but she seemed to be looking past him—past the doorway, past Samantha, straight through to something outside, something past their street, their neighbourhood. Beyond where the water began and all the way across it, through to another world.

"Open it up further. I know you ain't shy."

Somewhere, Grammy's voice. "Only pictures, mind."

"Yes, ma'am. Sure." The man raised a camera.

Retreating through the artificial dark, the tiles ice, outside, the grass blades like fork tines. Stumbling then running for the hog plum tree, clambering up quick, skin her shins in the scramble and don't feel.

It was a long minute that passed, without sound. Then clanking and banging, ugly metal noises, and finally, the washer raised its familiar hum, the sing of the motor, of water filling the tub. The back door opened. The man passed right under the tree and she froze, holding her breath. He looked up as he passed under anyway, looked up right at her like he knew she would be there. Whispered. Smiled, showing teeth. Too many of them, small and dull and stained brown. She squeezed her eyes shut as he moved beneath her, through the yard. When she opened her eyes, she could see him still. He was up the street, but she felt him watching her, from below, from close. Dingy yellow eyes, two rows of filthy teeth, tongue a slimy thing, pincer mouth, reaching.

Samantha began to draw. Slowly, carefully. Sudden moves might ruin everything. The sounds around her, pencils scratching over paper, the steady thump of Aaron kicking his desk's leg. Carefully, one broad, flat segment. Another, another, to four. On each, a fringe of twenty-five legs. She coloured them in, thick-pressed crayon, first dark brown, then stripes of red. She drew blades of grass, forked, green.

The morning seemed to stretch, extending for hours. Samantha drew Miss Ramsey, good wig on her head, yellow housecoat on, and barefoot, cutlass raised. She drew Debbie's eyes empty and wide, floating in the sky. Drew Debbie's skirt and blouse and feet. The hog plum tree. Herself in its shade, hiding, and a reddish, slick, slimy thing.

At last the bell rang, and around her, the children closed their books, passing them up to the front of the class, where Jillian stacked them on Mrs. Thompson's desk. Samantha stayed still, feeling the rush of movement around her as the children surged toward the door.

"May I have that?"

Samantha looked up. Mrs. Thompson stood over her, mouth slightly open in an almost-smile, just the right amount of teeth showing. Samantha flipped her cover closed.

"Can you hand your work to me?"

Samantha wanted to pull the book closer, secure it under her elbow, but her hands were occupied, fingers tracing the goosebumps along her arms. Mrs. Thompson made a sharp *hfff* through her nostrils as she took the book herself.

"Go on," she heard the teacher say. "It's recess. Go play."

∞

Mrs. Thompson thumbed through the books while she sipped at her coffee, enjoying the classroom's stillness. Anton, as usual, had written a nearly perfect piece about how the butterfly got its wings. Joey had not finished his work. Marie's story was utterly illegible. She would need to write it over as homework, if she could even decipher her own scrawl. Mrs. Thompson reached for Samantha's book. The girl had begun late, but had hunched over her page in complete silence for the last thirty minutes of class.

A whirl of colour slapped Mrs. Thompson in the face. No words, just markings in a thick, angry scrawl. The severed body of a centipede, piece here, piece there, a crudely drawn head. Pincers reaching their way out of a brown-toothed grin, yellow eyes staring out of the page. It was human— and not. A squatting woman, huge knife raised to strike again. And a—woman?—girl?—with a gaping shirt, the dots of two dark nipples scrawled onto her bare chest. Mrs. Thompson gasped, then slammed the book shut.

The classroom had grown warm. There was always one, at least, one child with a wild imagination, one whose parents let them watch horror movies, whose older siblings told ghost stories to them at night. In every class, one. And yet this was so specific, so strong, the crayon marks hard, angry on the page. It was so *real.*

Mrs. Thompson stood and opened the windows that overlooked the playground, one by one. There was the sandpit, with two or three of the boys from 4-P turning somersaults. Joey took a run, then launched himself into a flip, landing on his feet. His friends cheered. She looked for Samantha among the girls skipping, among the ones playing Red Light, Green Light near the equipment room wall. There she was, by the fence, alone. She saw the girl rub her hands over her arms as though brushing off some invisible prickly thing. Then the girl picked up a fallen poinciana pod and moved it, up, down, up, down, by her ear, as if to hear the seeds shift and sing.

∞

Samantha sat in the hog plum tree's leafy folds and caught the sun, but the metal cold stayed. She watched the man walk down the street's slow curve, his bag slung over his shoulder. He nodded a greeting at Mr. Munroe next door, who was washing his car. The man adapted his path to avoid a dog, its tail curled up so tight the tip stroked its haunch. As he neared Miss Ramsey's house, he raised an arm. Miss Ramsey straightened up, the cutlass still in her hand. She waved back.

Inside, Grammy called for her. Samantha glanced toward the house, pressing her back against the tree. The door opened and Grammy's head appeared, looking left, right. Called her name again, shook her head, closed the door. Samantha wrapped her arms around herself, hungry for warmth. She turned to the street.

The man was gone. She strained to see him, pulling herself to stand, pushing leaves out of the way. She had only looked away for a moment—he should have been just a little past Miss Ramsey's house now. Or still there—even in her yard. They had waved at each other. But Miss Ramsey was alone, squatting down again. She crouched forward and slashed into the grass with her cutlass, then jumped back, hollering.

"Centipee!" Miss Ramsey shrieked between hops, and Samantha could see it. Red-brown body, stained teeth, pincer slick. Miss Ramsey's arm worked fast, landing heavy, high strikes in the grass. She was slaughtering it—him. "Centipee! Centipee!"

∞

Mrs. Thompson moved back to her desk, shaking her head. She checked the calendar at the front of her attendance book. Turned nine last month. The older Butler girl, Debbie, had come through the primary school a few years before, raising clatter everywhere she went. A shoe-dragger, a screamer in hallways, a talker in class, a whisperer in tests, a weeper when her softball team lost, a mutterer of curse words, a caller-out of wrong answers, a singer of off-key notes, a vexation, a suck-teeth, a perpetual din. And if such things were possible, Mrs. Thompson would have sworn, that year Debbie was in her class, she could *hear* the girl bursting into puberty. Finally, flushed out of Saints of the Sanctuary's primary school and into the high school, she had become the problem of other teachers. Out of Mrs. Thompson's sight, Mrs. Pyfrom's sight, Mr. Andrews' (who had happened upon Debbie in the art room closet with a flashlight, another girl, and a shocking magazine most commonly found among bad ninth-grade boys), she had been fully out of mind. It was easy to forget her, even when teaching her sister. Samantha had never been anything like the older girl. Until now.

The rest of the books waited, unmarked. Mrs. Thompson walked over to the windows, raised a fist to knock. She hesitated. She didn't have to call the girl in. After the summer, Samantha would move on to another grade. Samantha—*no*. She had to talk to the girl. If she'd stepped in with Debbie, perhaps the younger sister wouldn't be here now, drawing these—aberrations.

"Samantha!" Mrs. Thompson banged on the metal window frame. "Jillian! Jillian, call Samantha over here!" From the playground, Jillian peered at her through the window slats, puzzled. "Over by the fence. Go tell her I said come in."

∞

In the relative privacy of the playground's edge, Samantha shook the poinciana pod harder, as though that would warm her body. Shaken, it made a sound like controlled rain, though it was muffled, faraway. She put her pod on the ground, stood on it with one foot, and began to bend it.

"Humph." Miss Ramsey made a sound of satisfaction as she dropped the cutlass in the grass. She stood up, dusting her hands off. Her eyes picked Samantha out of the tree. "Sammy! Sammy, you see I kill him, ay?"

Samantha didn't answer. She felt the insides of her cheeks begin to water, and swallowed the saliva down, forcing herself not to throw up. And yet, beneath the nausea that threatened to overwhelm her, was a bitter, shameful relief.

The back door opened and Debbie stuck her head out. The sun was angled and over-bright. Debbie shaded her eyes as she stepped outside. She had on a fresh cotton t-shirt, soft blue. She balanced a laundry basket on one hip, full of wet clothes.

"Grammy callin' you."

Her sister's voice should have sounded different.

"What she want?" Samantha asked. She braced herself for another wave of chills; she would have to go inside.

"Go ask her yourself." The same old Debbie voice, flat and bored.

"He inside?" Samantha asked, even though she knew he was not. A part of her needed to feel sure, to see, with some certainty, what she knew had happened to him.

Debbie let the door bang behind her, sauntered over toward the clothesline. Dumped down the hamper, shook out a clean pillowcase, pinned its corners to the wire. Her fingers moved quickly, sure of themselves, shaking out the damp laundry piece by piece. "Only Grammy inside. You crazy, eh? What you talking fool for?"

Samantha lifted the poinciana pod. It was whole, still, but the shape was warped so it looked like a boomerang.

"Hey. Hey!" Someone was shouting at her. Jillian, sharp and skinny and quick. Samantha had looked over at Jillian during Mamma Ramsey's lie-story and seen how the girl leaned forward, chin in her hand, listening like the words were ice cream being dropped down her throat.

Samantha regarded her classmate with suspicion.

"Teacher call you."

She turned away from Jillian and began to shake the pod harder, trying to drown out her voice.

"You ain' goin'? She call you, she right up there." Jillian pointed up toward the classroom. The windows were tipped partly open, but it was impossible to see anything inside from so far away.

Samantha looked away from the girl, shook her pod. Its rattle was reassuringly loud over Jillian's words.

"Teacher call you, you ain' hear me?"

"Go away."

"You in trouble."

"That's a lie."

"Don't believe me, then."

"I don't. And that story in assembly was a lie too."

"Shut up, you big head," Jillian flung back as she flounced away.

Samantha longed to call an insult after her. A small pain had begun to open up in her stomach. She sidled toward the school door, the sun bouncing off her skin as she went. Once inside, she hid in the nook at the end of the grade four classrooms, by the stairs, waiting for the first bell to ring.

∞

Mrs. Thompson had gone on marking the other stories while she waited for Samantha to come inside. *Once upon a time, a princess. Once, a toad and a frog.* The electric bell rang, heralding the five-minute warning before recess would end. Where was Samantha? The girl was Debbie all over again. Mrs. Thompson stood up, stretched, wondering whether she should bring Samantha's book with her when she went out to meet the children. No. It would look suspicious if she had only one. She pushed her chair in, snaked through the rows of desks, some sloppy, some neat, and went out to gather her children in.

∞

The classroom was empty. Samantha moved inside. There was her exercise book, crisp on the table, edges still unrumpled, free of finger smudges. She tore out the pages, one, two, then shoved her book underneath all the others. When she was done, she hurried out onto the playground, reaching it just as the old bell was rung, *clang-a-lang-a-lang*, ending playtime.

∞

"Alright, class," Mrs. Thompson said, once the children had filed into the classroom, "I want everyone to quietly— *quietly*—turn to page 90 in the reading comprehension book and read the story entitled 'A Magical Walk Home.'" When they were settled, she beckoned Samantha up to her desk.

"I looked at the work you did this morning." She reached for the book. It was not on the top where she had left it. She lifted the neat stack, flipping through the books. "Didn't you hand in your book, Samantha?"

The girl shrugged. Even before she had finished the shrug, her arms had again crossed over her chest, hands rubbing opposite arms. The gesture made Mrs. Thompson want to smack her. Couldn't she just stand up straight?

Mrs. Thompson found the book at the very bottom of the pile. She tossed it down on the desk and it fell open, bare pages laid out guiltily before them both.

"But I saw it. I saw what you did. Where did it go?"

The girl's hands moved up, down, up, down, from her elbows to her wrists, faster, faster, as though at any moment a spark might catch and she'd ignite right there in front of Mrs. Thompson's desk. Mrs. Thompson looked away. She could not think why the child's movements irritated her so.

"You'll stay in at lunch and do it again. And do it properly," she said sharply.

When Samantha was settled at her own desk, Mrs. Thompson breathed out a sigh. She'd tried, but what could she do? She couldn't help something that had disappeared. Better to just let the girl start fresh.

At the end of the day, Samantha returned her book to Mrs. Thompson. The girl must have been ashamed; she kept her eyes low, her face blank. The teacher paused before flipping open the cover. A centipede snaked many times around a disproportionately small house. A tree, a girl in it, another girl in front of the house. Both girls clothed, thankfully. The house bulged slightly, as though constricted by the centipede's body. It was childishly irrelevant, connected to the actual assignment only closely enough to be minimally acceptable. Mrs. Thompson looked up to speak to the child, but she had disappeared.

∞

"Don't you worry." His whisper floated up through the leaves and hung there beside her like past-ripe fruit. "I see you ain't ready yet. Next time, baby. See you next time. Real soon."

∞

Mrs. Thompson packed the last exercise book into her bag. As she stood to go, she saw the girl lingering outside the classroom, alone.

"Go on, time to go home," Mrs. Thompson said. "Tomorrow's a new day."

When the child didn't move, Mrs. Thompson brushed by, annoyed. "Bring a sweater tomorrow since you're always so cold."

∞

Samantha reached into the garbage under the teacher's desk for the two crumpled pages shoved at the bottom. She stuffed them into her knapsack and strapped the bag onto her shoulders.

Outside, the sun had weakened. She began down the path to the parking lot to meet Debbie so they could walk home together. She saw her sister coming toward her then, flanked by two friends. One of them said something that made Debbie stop, look behind her, tip her head back, and spill laughter forth, heavy, warm. The laugh was like a broken sail, half secured and half loose, flapping toward the sky. It caught on the wind and hovered above them, dancing on the air. Samantha opened up her arms and ran toward her, eager for her share.

MORNING SWIM

THE MORNING WALKS HAD NOT WORKED. If they had, Renee would not have been there in the doctor's office, holding a slick brochure in one hand, the other hand tucked under her right breast. The brochure was produced in the States. On the front was a picture of a slender white woman half her age staring expectantly, almost worshipfully, at a doctor with an expression of arrogant sympathy on his face. The woman was draped in a saggy blue blouse, designed, it seemed, to eliminate any suggestion of curves. It was loose enough to smuggle a pineapple underneath.

Every morning for the past eight months, Renee had gone for a walk at six thirty. She had slipped out of bed with care, though Ellis slept like death. She had splashed water on her face, brushed her teeth, stroked deodorant on, and donned aqua spandex shorts, a blue sports bra, sneakers, and a clean t-shirt and socks. She had strapped on her cheap digital watch, locked her sleeping family inside the house, and set out for the sea.

Four minutes down the main road, Renee would reach the drugstore and glance at her newly athletic self in the window panes. She would admire the roundness of her bottom and breasts, undisguised by the fitness gear. She would feel briefly annoyed that her belly had not shrunk. Six minutes later, she would cross over to the other side of the street, where she would pass the abandoned maroon car that had been parked in an empty lot overgrown with bush since the previous summer, morning glories twining around its wheels. About ten minutes later, she would see the first potcake, dozing under a large poinciana tree. It usually twitched an ear, raised its head and one eyebrow, then laid back down in the dust. At some point during the next eight to twelve minutes, depending on whether she was feeling spritely or weary, Renee would encounter the other, more aggressive potcake, who often required the use of a stick to discourage his nipping overtures. She would meet a fellow walker who was on her way back from the sea wall, a large house that made Renee's seem like a shack, two small children walking to the bus stop, a young woman in blue scrubs, and a 15A bus heading into town. Early on in her walking days, Renee had noted the fellow walker, a royal palm of a woman, tall and straight and sculpted, each part held proud and perfectly in place, been awed by how she moved her arms vigorously in an exaggerated stride, pumping them like a Defence Force officer. "Keeps my heart rate up," the woman had called out, answering an unspoken question. Renee began to pump her arms up and down as well, and this, too, became part of the routine.

∞

"Have you told your family about the procedure yet?" Renee's doctor asked. She was shorter than Renee by a few inches, and about fifteen years younger. It unsettled Renee, being cared for by someone her junior. Today, they were in a different room. The walls were peach, a strangely intimate tone that made Renee think of the palms of her children's hands, of holding those hands, inspecting them, when, as small girls, she had clipped their nails.

Renee swallowed to make room in her mouth for the lie. "Of course. Yes."

The doctor nodded, her lips pressed together in a grim smile, and continued, describing what would have to be done. Renee nodded too, as though she agreed. She was not sure what, exactly, she was consenting to with this mirrored movement—she only knew that something in her wanted, instead, to shake her head.

∞

At the shore, Renee always stopped, shed her shoes and socks, and stepped barefoot onto the sand. She thought about how much she would enjoy a swim. She dabbled her feet in the shallows, wiggled her toes, admired the smooth shell-curve of her toenails. She watched the woman who lived across the road from the beach come out and sweep down her doorstep, watched the custodian for the church pull into the yard, mouth moving with the unconsidered rhythm of a herding animal as he chewed the last of his breakfast. After ten minutes, she would sigh, brush off her feet, put on both socks and shoes, and walk back. Usually she made it back in twenty-five minutes, urged home by the grains between her toes.

∞

The doctor was staring at Renee, her mouth closed, lips pressed tight into a frown. She seemed to be waiting for some sort of response.

"Of course." It seemed a low-risk thing to say.

"Renee? Are you sure?"

"Unless you . . . advise otherwise."

The doctor glanced at a point just above Renee's head. Renee turned. There was nothing behind her, only the door, and above that, the clock. 4:35. She had been here more than half an hour.

"Well, if that's all, then, I'll see you on Monday at 8 a.m."

The doctor spoke as though it was Renee's first day at a new job. First project: tumour removal.

Renee nodded.

"And Renee?" the doctor said as Renee was halfway out of the door. "Make sure you bring someone with you on the day."

All the way down the hall, she rehearsed the conversation she would have—already should have had—with Ellis. *They found—the mass is*—but at the word, she always stopped short. Back in the car, she started up, and the radio blared back into life along with the engine, a parasite unexpectedly revived.

"—immigrants intercepted in waters off the southern tip of Inagua." The newscaster's voice was calm; no matter what she was reporting, her tone was always calm. "The migrants included sixteen men and—"

Renee snapped the news off and leaned back into the headrest, closing her eyes. She could feel her body, heavy in the seat, the press of bone and flesh into the cloth upholstery, but she still felt loose, as though some other, less sturdy part of herself had been unhooked and might, without warning, drift away.

∞

"How was the doctor?" Ellis stretched his legs out under the table, shifting. His sock-shrouded toes brushed against her bare ones. She moved away, reached for his empty plate. In the kitchen, her younger daughter clattered clean glasses into the top cupboard with less care than Renee would have liked.

"Grace, don't chip up my cups, please."

"It's not even my turn tonight," the girl answered, banging the cupboard door closed.

"Renee?"

That night, she would wonder why she answered, *Good. Everything's clear.* She lay beside Ellis, curled facing him, listening to the soft huff and pull of his breath. She raised one hand level with her face and closed, then opened, her eyes, but either way, she could see nothing before her but the night.

∞

6:47 Monday morning, Renee sat up, unable to lie there awake any longer. It would only take fifteen minutes to get to the hospital, another five to park. She didn't need more than ten minutes to dress and shower. But her body was ready for what it knew. It wanted to walk as it did every morning, wanted to feel calves and thighs, stiff from the night's stagnation, slowly warming to motion. Ellis lay on his back, mouth open, snoring like a drill on concrete. In the closet, Renee's hand hovered just in front of the peach blouse and tan pants she had pressed the night before. Something made her draw back, step away. Turn to the bureau and draw out her everyday clothes; shorts, oversized shirt, sports bra underneath. She dressed, then tiptoed past the room where the girls slept, and stepped out.

She unlocked her car, took a moment to lift her left hand to her right, steadying her slight shake, then slid into the driver's seat. 7:05. Renee started the car up and drove to the end of her street. She should turn right at the main road, toward town, toward the hospital. Almost without choice, she signalled left instead, then swung onto the main road, toward the shore.

It surprised her, how quickly she moved past her usual landmarks. All the same characters were there, but driving her route shifted everything. As the car moved past the pharmacy, she glimpsed its sleek form distorted in the glass. The first potcake yawned but did not bother to raise its head. The second dog barked, trotting after the car to nip at its wheels, its run ungainly and lopsided. In the rearview mirror, she saw that its teats were distended. Renee shuddered as the dog gave a final yip, then turned and trotted back to its tree.

At the sea wall, Renee stopped the car, got out, and sat. The beach was empty. The churchyard sat vacant, the house across the road still asleep, curtains drawn tight. 7:12.

To the south, boats tied up outside the walls of the oceanfront houses bobbed and nodded in private agreement.

Renee removed her sneakers and socks, then dropped her keys into the toe of the left shoe. The sand gave way under her feet, obedient. She lingered at the edge; the tide seemed perfectly balanced, neither coming in nor receding. Renee looked down at her bare feet—the stubby toes, carefully clipped nails, the slightly hardened heels, all softened, somehow, by the damp. Then she stepped in. The sea was cool, as though it had retained some of the night. It woke her. Made her feel alive. She should dry off her feet. She should turn back, drive home. Shower quickly, shake Ellis awake, whisper to him about the appointment, the surgery. Brave his shock, then his hurt. Dress in a shapeless blouse and skirt, a good pair of panties and matching bra, let him drive her down to the hospital, wait. But what would it be like to be out on one of those boats? Slipping onto the cool plastic seats, leaving the motor off, just untethering, letting it drift? Nowhere to go, to be, just bobbing along, the strange shift and rock of the waves, nothing solid underneath.

Renee pulled off the t-shirt and dropped it onto the sand. She stepped deeper into the water, knee-deep. It was warm. Renee kept moving in; the sea clung to her, heavy and thick. The beach was silent. Waist-deep, now. Renee contemplated lying back in the water, floating as she had done as a little girl when her father had taken her and her brothers to the beach before school, or in the evenings after he returned from a day on the water. She could not think of an excuse she could give the surgeon for turning up at the hospital with wet hair, her body gritty from salt and sand.

Something made Renee look over, further out. The circling of a gull, a shift, a school of shadows deeper in. Fish, rocks, water moving. She looked up, then down, before her eyes came to focus on the low boat. It rocked, untied and too close to shore. There was no dock nearby, only a reef that stretched out as far as she could see on the north side of the beach. It was too shallow to sail, too rocky to walk to. The boat was a hollow barely cresting, slung low, no interruption of a motor. It must have been painted blue; it shifted in and out of sight with the rocking of waves. There was no reason for it to be there. Renee took a deep breath and leaned forward, putting her face into the salt water, lifting her feet off the sea bottom. Letting go.

It had been years; her arms and legs struggled for familiarity. Then she found it, the salt holding her body as she relaxed, as if it were a familiar lover. She moved through, parting it with her hands, pushing forward and out, legs frog-kicking behind her. Without thought, her limbs selected her old swimming style moments before her mind registered the irony: breaststroke. Her heart thumped but her movements were sure and calm, as though they belonged to some other, more reliable body. The boat was closer, closer, each time she surfaced. Renee paused and looked down at her watch. It was not waterproof. Moisture was already seeping in, the digital numbers distorted into a jumble of shapes.

She was almost there, now, and she could see it was not a functional boat. It was too flat, sat too low in the water. Turquoise paint had chipped off the sides, exposing decayed wood underneath. It would be fully underwater by noon. She glanced down for a moment and was surprised to see that her legs had remembered how to tread water. Below her, the sand seemed far away. Her chest grew tight, heart pounding. The feeling was familiar and right, this tightness from being nervous about things that should cause nervousness. A half-sunken rowboat. Swimming in deep water with legs too used to land. Fear of what might lurk in the seagrass beneath.

Renee held her breath a moment, then struggled out of her sports bra. Her breasts remained squashed down at first, then slowly began to breathe out into their full form. Buoyed by the water, they bobbed, upright and free. She held the bra briefly, watching it waft and drift, anchored by her fingers, then released it, blue into blue, letting the waves lift and lower it out of sight. She reached over and held her right breast. Her fingers found the familiar hard place near her underarm. Then she pulled her hand away, wiped her face, and dipped her head back under. Her chest was tight. It was only from nervousness, she told herself. Nervousness because of the deep water. And there was no need for that, she had grown up by the sea. She knew it well. She pushed on. Stroke, breath, stroke, breath, over and over. Then she was there.

The boat was small. No longer than a dining table, no wider across. Water had pooled in the bottom already. Inside lay two people, flat, face up.

"Hello?" Her voice came out constricted, as though something was squeezing her throat from inside. The people—a man, a woman—were still. No. Stiff. Renee's own breath stopped. She felt, for a moment, that she, too, stopped, all of her. But her legs continued dancing through the water of their own accord.

They were whole; no cuts, no bruises. Their faces seemed young—smooth, still, and thin. Perhaps a little younger than she and Ellis had been when they met. The man's right hand hung down toward the bottom of the boat, fingers stiff. The fingers of his other hand curled around the woman's wrist. The woman's dress protruded unnaturally at the top, as though her bosom had been stuffed with something precious she had wanted to take with her into this new life. Her hair was tied down under a faded blue scarf that was knotted at the front the same way Renee secured hers at night. One arm was propped under the protrusion on her chest. It seemed like a compulsive gesture, a thing the woman had done hundreds of times, and had but crafted to look casual. At any moment, Renee expected the woman to lower her arm again. The edge of a plait poked out from under the scarf and dangled into the water that was collecting in the bottom of the boat. There was a moment where Renee envied the woman. She was gone; she didn't have to look at this. And Renee was here, and could not make herself do anything but see.

Movement, a small shifting, on the woman's chest. Startled, Renee lurched back, lost her grip. The water closed over her head for a moment, and as she looked up, the ocean sky seemed so far away. Then she was in air, gasping, coughing. She grabbed hold of the boat and peered inside again. More movement, and a sound, a mewing, perhaps a gull. Renee closed her eyes. Heat on her lids; too early for such a burn on her skin. The feeling strange: her chest bare and yet, a tightening, as though something in her might implode. She had to open her eyes. Above, a seagull circled, raising its call. In the distance, another answered. Renee reached into the boat, pulled back the top of the woman's dress.

A tiny bundle, wrapped in discoloured cloth. Barely moving, eyes half open, chest to chest with the woman, face toward her, looking. Baby. No. Oh, no. Renee clasped the boat's edge, wet wood under her fingers. Then the baby moved a small arm.

Renee reached over, one hand steadying—the boat could tip any moment, and it seemed like the stability of the entire world depended on this not happening. She could not lose this baby—and the man and woman could not be disturbed.

She had to give them at least this. Reach, reach, she was almost overbalancing, and—skin under hers, and firm, and warm. She had it, had the baby, held under one of its arms, precarious, slippery. She let go of the boat and it righted, a wash of ocean surging in, over them. Renee clung to the baby and turned for the shore. She had to keep going. She tried to swim on her back, the baby lifted above her chest, but her legs refused to propel her. She struggled against the waves as she clasped the baby with one arm, half floating, half treading water. The baby recoiled, setting up a hoarse cry as the waves touched it. The baby's eyes found hers as it wailed. Renee felt herself starting to shake, and manoeuvred herself around in the water, keeping the baby above the surface. There was no choice. She had to dog paddle, with one arm. Slowly, she turned and began to pull herself through the water using her right arm and her legs. With the left arm, she held onto the baby. The shore was far.

Once, Renee glanced down. Seaweed fluttered far below her. The baby was quiet now. Its small insides beat against her. Then the sand was rising, slowly, slowly, to her toes, to her feet, and she eased the baby into her arms properly. Then she was stepping down fully, running through deep, then shallower, then shallow water, barely hearing the splashes. Then her legs remembered, and nearly gave way. No, she told her body. Not done yet. Still more.

"It's okay," Renee tried to say, and coughed up seawater. She held her chest a moment, then kept moving. There was her t-shirt on the dry sand. She lunged for it, let herself sit. Unstrapped the swollen diaper, lifted the baby free. She wrapped her—it was a girl—in the dry shirt. Her own breath was settling, slowly. Chest opening. She could almost breathe properly. She reached for her shoes, found the keys inside. She half-ran to the car, opened the door. Heat belched out of the vehicle and she rolled the windows down, then got in. The driver's seat felt strange, as though it was a portal back to reality from some other strange land.

The girl gave a weak cry as Renee fumbled for the ignition. She started up the car. In Renee's arms, the baby turned her head, searching for warmth. Renee had to go. As she swung onto the road, she tried to recall what she had in the fridge. She could picture the jug of water, a bottle of juice. Was she out of milk? She slowed the car at her turn-off, easing into the middle of the road to wait for a break in the traffic. In the crook of her arm, the baby moved again, tiny mouth opening against Renee's breast. She was too weak to cry.

The bus coming toward her flashed its lights, the driver waving her on to turn ahead of him, urging her home. She looked up. First she saw annoyance, then the shocked O of his mouth, and she wondered if he could see the baby in her lap, then remembered she was bare. Then she was pulling away from him, back into traffic, toward the hospital. *Don't die*, she prayed. *Don't die.*

GLORY

PRISCILLA STEPPED OFF THE MAILBOAT and looked around to see if God was on the dock. She stood amongst the push of fat women shouting to the men onboard about this package or that box their cousin or sister or friend had sent from Nassau, and felt in her pocket for the letter her mother had given her for Grammy. She had snuck and read it on the boat. It spent the first two lines praising God's majesty and greatness and the last two hoping the hand of God was still as strong on the island as ever. In between were several sentences lamenting Priscilla and what was inside her and, less explicitly, what had been inside her, and expressing hope that Priscilla would Repent And Find God. The girl searched the shore for signs of a celestial presence. Lanky casuarinas lined the water. Beyond lurked dirt road, bush, low roofs.

"'Scuse me." A woman stepped off the boat and swept past Priscilla in a glorious whirl of nutmeg and fabric the colour of plums. Priscilla was intrigued; the woman was worlds apart from the figures jostling for their deliveries in stretched-out yellowed t-shirts and mismatched shapeless skirts. She wanted to call after the woman, to hurry after her, to step into her life instead. But then Grammy, who she had not seen since she was six, appeared at her elbow and seized her arm, and the woman was gone.

"I see ya showin' already," the old woman muttered, guiding Priscilla roughly through the jangle of tongues and elbows onto proper land and toward a broke-down taxi with a jowly patriarch dozing at the wheel. "Drive us up by me, Mr. Bethel. I ga pay you tomorrow." Grammy glanced at the girl's sleeveless top, jeans hung low on her hips, and shook her head. She was none too pleased at having yet another grandchild sent to pass the rest of her time of shame in the little blue house.

"This another one a the grands, eh?" Mr. Bethel heaved himself to a more upright posture and struggled the car to a start.

"Inez's youngest. Come to stay out the summer." Grammy pressed her lips together. "Ain' even fifteen yet, an bring shame on herself already."

∞

A dusty rooster and a badly tuned radio woke Priscilla just before six. She rolled over, then sat up. First sun strained at the spare room's thin curtains. Through the open door, Priscilla could hear the old woman in the other room, grunting herself upright. Priscilla lay down again and stuffed her head under the lumpy pillow, the worn cotton sheet scratchy against her face. On the radio, a woman dragged out the last chords of "To God Be the Glory" with the victory and cheer of a funeral march.

"Up you get, ain' no time to be layin' around in bed."

Pricilla froze—how did the old woman get in here so silently? Before she could ponder this deeply, Grammy pulled the sheet away.

"This a place you earn ya keep. Ya ma ain' sen you up here fa no vacation," she announced, striding toward the bathroom.

Priscilla continued to lie in bed, bemused. The old woman seemed human—right now, she was in the bathroom, gargling like a mortal, as though she had not just spirited herself silently into Priscilla's room to haul her into wakefulness. Grammy spat. At the sound of the toilet seat clacking open, Priscilla pulled herself upright. She walked through the living room to the front door, then let herself out and stepped barefoot through the thin crabgrass sidewinding across the yard's dirt. The air smelled salty and clean, none of the lingering exhaust fumes she sometimes caught a whiff of, back home. She lay down on the low concrete wall that separated Grammy's property from the street. A light breeze kicked up, blowing dawn in. Daylight swelled like her rising belly. She closed her eyes. The warm air cupped her stomach, and the child inside her kicked a shooting star.

Inside, Grammy turned the fire out under the Cream of Wheat. "Child, I ain' know where you is, but ya better come get this food while it hot, cause I ain' gat the strength to call for you." She banged a mug down on the counter and poured out her morning tea. "Oh, Glory." Another day. Another girl done got herself in trouble. Nothing new under the moon nor the sun. She caught sight of the girl's shoes by the kitchen door. Not even as big as her own shoes, foot ain' even half grow yet. How these girls get theyself in this kind a mess? She shook her head, glanced through the kitchen window, and nearly scalded herself at the sight. Her granddaughter, laid out flat on the wall like a common creeping vine, shirt hauled up almost to the chest, her sin exposed in a small brown dome. "Lord Father, grant me goodness and patience." This one was a real she-devil, not satisfy with one baby, out tryin' to catch more attention. Come to test her salvation. "Priscilla!" Grammy's voice rang out through the waking street.

∞

"Grammy, you think stars shoot in the daytime?"

The old woman thumped at the wad of dough. "Bay leaf in the soup yet?"

Priscilla poked two leaves into the pot, then peeled a pair of onions, washed and chopped them. On the radio, the eleven o'clock news began; two murders in the capital overnight, a possible strike at the water company, gas prices going up again.

"Lord, so much wickedness in this place." The old woman heaved the dough up, turned it, then punched it down as if it had offended her.

"I never saw a shooting star. Grammy, you ever see God? I never saw Him. I think we don' see cause we ain' got no mountains." Priscilla pushed the onions into the pot. They made a small splash on the stovetop and the burner sizzled in protest. "God like mountains, you know. I don' think God would stay in a place that don' have no mountains."

The old woman pressed her lips together, shook her head.

"Grammy, why you think we ain' got no mountains here? It so flat. I mean, Jamaica have, an Trinidad have, an Saint Lucia an Saint Vincent an—"

"You better get your life right an pray one day you could be on the right side a ya Saviour to ask Him these fool questions."

"Or Her." She dug out the core of a green pepper, spilling white seeds onto the counter.

"Lord Jesus, *grant* me the patience." Grammy began chopping the dough with a viciousness that would have made her husband cringe, had he still been alive. "Peel the carrots, hear?"

There were a few minutes of near-silence, backgrounded only by the *ssshhhk ssshhhk* of knife through vegetable. Then: "Grammy, how big you think I ga get?"

The old woman banged the knife down on the counter. "Ya too womanish. You ain' business askin' them questions. In my day, if a girl got herself take advantage of, she knew not to talk about it an certainly not to show it off. Layin' around outside wid ya shame expose. Shame on you." She began batting at the rolls with an eggy pastry brush. "Try hard season that soup right. Lord knows ya ma never teach you to cook."

Priscilla stirred at the pot. Sticks of thyme floated inside like long insect legs. If Grammy knew the answers to these questions about what would happen in the coming months, why wouldn't she share them?

"Auntie Bessa-Mae live far from here?"

The old woman slammed the rolls into the oven. "Far enough."

Priscilla opened her mouth to ask if Aunt Esther lived nearby, even though her mother had forbidden her to mention that name. She looked over at her grandmother, face pressed into a persistent scowl. Priscilla thought better of it, and closed her mouth.

44

When the peas had been added to the pot and the soup was bubbling on the back burner, Priscilla said, "Grammy, I could go down to the water this evening?"

Evening? the old woman thought. "Ain' safe to go out close to dark round here." She shot up a hasty prayer, repenting for the lie. "You better go soon, after the food cook an you help me carry it out to Miss Darlene car. An when you go, keep ya clothes on for once, an mind you don' pick up nobody to talk to."

Thank you, Jesus, she thought an hour later, as she watched the girl carry the last basket of rolls out to the neighbour's rickety station wagon, then make her way down the road to the sea.

∞

The sea wall had been badly broken down twelve or so storm seasons back, and since it did not directly face the tall houses on the side of the island where visitors and rich people stayed, there had never been much of a push to fix it. Priscilla found a stretch of concrete long enough to lay out on, under the shade of a large tree she could not name, with small, dark leaves and branches that eagerly spread up and out. Her mother had promised to call again that night. She still hadn't grown tired of asking Priscilla who she had got herself pregnant with. Priscilla hadn't felt like giving a response yet. Besides, it was more interesting to think up answers to the questions her own daughter would have.

As if on cue, the baby kicked. "What you wan', you?" *You* wasn't a very good name. "What you wan' me name you?" It—she—kicked again. It had to be a girl. She would come out a light brown, and would grow up to like dancing and strong sun and going to church just to sing. She would want to know where the mountains were around here, how to measure nighttime in handfuls. Maybe God would show up before the baby came, so Priscilla could get some real answers.

Grammy had said something about going to church, an experience Priscilla dreaded. She vaguely remembered her last visit here, tight black shoes squeezing her feet as she sat beside her grandmother in the pew. On both of the walls on either side of her, dour, pale Jesuses held out empty hands. The pastor droned from the pulpit, and appeared to be nodding off himself between verses. If God planned to show up, it likely wouldn't be there, except perhaps for a nap.

"I see you found the right place."

Priscilla sat up so fast she hit her head on a low branch. She grabbed at the wall, steadying herself.

"Don't fall now," the same voice said.

A woman, though Priscilla couldn't see who. She brought her hand to her forehead.

"You hit yourself too hard the baby ga come out stupid. Lay down catch yourself."

Firm hands pushed her back into a recline. The stone was a comfort beneath her.

"Close ya eyes before you get dizzy." The advice was good, but late. "Let me give you something for your head, you got a little cut." The woman pressed something soft to Priscilla's skin, just above her left eyebrow. Cloth buttery smooth. Warm, as if it had been close to the woman's body a moment earlier. The woman moved one of Priscilla's hands up to hold it in place.

"It's okay, this baby strong," the woman said. "I could tell."

Priscilla opened one eyelid carefully. The sky was still blue; a wisp of pine needles nodded in and out of view with the breeze. A puff of the woman's shirt floated up, then drifted away.

"So what you doin' here in the middle of the day?"

Priscilla shrugged, then realized how uncomfortable the motion was when done while lying on concrete.

"You don't know what you come here for?"

Priscilla's scattered thoughts slowly began to come together. Who was this person? Why was she rattling off questions? The way she had materialized reminded her of Grammy. Perhaps it was an island trait.

"You hear me?" the woman needled.

"Just thinkin'." Priscilla was still woozy; she couldn't quite grab hold of her words enough to quiz this woman in return. Another flutter of cloth—it was a tan print, one of those designs that were meant to look African.

"About?"

"I dunno. I guess, life." She shifted slightly to get comfortable. "Just meditating."

"Well, the island is a good place to meditate. How long you plan on meditating for?"

"Just the afternoon."

"I mean how long you in town for?"

"Oh." That. "Four months." She realized she had moved her free hand onto her stomach. "Or so."

There was a pause before the woman said, "I see," then asked, "you still dizzy?"

No, she thought, but tiredness was creeping over her quick. She wanted to ask the woman what her name was. She closed her eyes.

When Priscilla woke, the trees were making long shadows. The sun had grown gold, and she could not, for some moments, remember clearly where she was. The day's heat had eased. Above her head, the guilty branch observed her. She sat up, slowly this time, and a light purple scarf slipped off her midsection. It was spotted slightly with red. Her head ached. She was alone. She folded up the scarf and set it down on the wall, then reconsidered, tucked it under her arm, and headed back to the little blue house.

∞

Midday was by far the best time to come to the beach. In the morning, old people came for their daily swim. Her grandmother was not amongst them. Evenings, a handful of people drifted by after work. Later, a few pairs would show up, hand in hand. In the middle of the day, Priscilla had the beach to herself.

She lay down on the sand and began to build a sand belly on top of her real one. The structure grew, firm and heavy. The sand under her was tightly packed and comfortable. She poked a finger into the sand belly, a few inches below the crest, and made a large, hollow navel.

"Careful you don' wash out to sea."

Priscilla craned her neck. Behind her, a little ways off in the water, was a woman. She thought she recognized her voice.

The woman was nothing special to look at, and was wearing far too much for someone in the water: a sleeveless shirt, and a long skirt that fanned out around her in the sea. She stood almost as tall as Grammy, but not quite, and was one of those miscellaneous brown shades that was neither light enough to glean favour nor dark enough to warrant haughtiness about being undiluted. She was a little solid, maybe. She squinted against the sun. Priscilla pushed the sand belly off, feeling foolish, and slowly sat up. Her head seemed to take a moment to catch her body.

"I don't think your baby would like that. Or your grammy. You layin' back in the sand. Never wash all a that out your head. Bring half the beach onto her good sheets."

It sounded very much like what her grandmother would say. "You know my grammy?"

"What you doin' here today? Meditating again?"

Priscilla disliked the way the woman seemed not to hear her question. She stood up and walked past her and into the water. She immersed herself, sand and bubbles dispersing through the clear. A muffled sound as the water closed over her head. She stood up, clearing eyes, clearing ears. Water clung to her hair, heavy. The woman was gone.

∞

There was so little to do on the island besides help Grammy in the kitchen, walk down to the dock or over to Grey's store and between the three narrow aisles of dimly lit cans and dusty bags of rice and flour. Grammy reminded Priscilla about Wednesday night Bible Study, but didn't push when the girl claimed a headache. "Suit yaself," she called as she left, "see, I leavin' my spare Bible here, maybe you could read something an learn." No response came. *Peace and solitude*, the old woman thought, as she let the screen door close behind her.

The island houses were not as quiet as Priscilla had

expected. On one side, now, a neighbour's radio blasted the news on the crackly AM station. It was hot in the house, stuffy. Priscilla turned off the dining room light and went out to sit on the front porch. She would hear the radio wherever she was, anyway; she might as well get some breeze. The neighbour waved from her own porch, so close she could almost have brushed the side of Grammy's house, and fumbled to change the station to a broadcast from a Nassau congregation. The radio service opened with a greeting from the pastor. His voice was familiar—a higher voice for a man, and strident. "And the Lawd said," he began, with the raspy tone he always gave his sermons in, "make a joyful noise unto the Lawd, for wonders He hath done, Praise God!"

The neighbour's "Amen!" echoed those that came from the box. She twiddled the dial, and the sound came clearer now. The choir started up with "Faith of Our Fathers." Priscilla laughed to herself because the whole choir sounded like women.

"That's Mary grand there, eh?" the neighbour called over to her, when the singing had finished and the organist was improvising an elaborate bridge. "Ya grammy gone to her worship service, eh? I havin' my own hallelujah right here in my house clothes. Jesus in my slippers. Can't beat that, eh?"

Priscilla began to answer, but the neighbour struck up a chord then, obliterating the band.

After the hymn, a deacon began reading announcements. The neighbour, taking this as an ad break, dipped inside.

Singing recommenced. The song was not one Priscilla knew, but it was full of dragging notes, sloping up, up, up, then dropping dangerous, sudden, then shifting gradually up again like a lazy hill that almost couldn't be bothered to rise. Her eyes were heavy. Priscilla turned to go back inside and tripped over a heavy book. "I tired a this place!" She knew she said it, but the neighbour—from the bathroom, it sounded, from the echo and hollow—had rejoined the choir, and she could not hear her own words. Priscilla grabbed up the book—her fingers found it before she even noticed which it was—and flung it. It sailed across the yard and hit the radio; there was a crash, then another. The choir vanished. Static fuzz.

"Frankie! What I tell you bout messin' with my radio?" The neighbour's toilet flushed. Priscilla ducked and scurried off the porch and through the front yard. She flew down the path, around the corner, out of sight. Her feet took her to the water.

It was dark and, further from the houses, quiet, quiet, quiet. Land valleyed toward wet. She had forgotten her shoes. Pavement road, rocky rough. Tiny cones, pointed, round, mixed with pine needles silk smooth. Salt air. She inhaled, sucked it in. Moonless. Ocean, sky, leave off where? Then sand, dry, grooved, giving, up, down, tumble easy to new ups, downs. Then, where water broke, cool sand, sturdy firm. She could not see the prints she knew were there. The waves were small.

Splash, further out. Priscilla froze, called out, but the noise that came from her mouth was wordless, strange. Her tongue was heavy with fear. Her stomach jolted. She covered it with her hands. The splashing stopped. Priscilla stepped back lightly, wet hard sand, then dry, then needles again.

"Who's that?" The voice that came was fearless and sure, somehow.

Priscilla cleared her throat. "Priscilla." She paused. "And my baby."

"You come to swim, eh?"

"Just for quiet." It was that same woman again. Who else would it be? Priscilla's chest calmed. She kept her hands on her middle.

"Can't come to the beach an don swim. That's like goin' to dinner just to talk."

Priscilla faintly remembered something about swimming at night and the number of sharks and stingrays that came close to the shore after dark.

"If it wasn't safe, you think I'd be in here?" the woman said, reading her thoughts. "But I guess your grammy might not like it."

The water was warm around Priscilla's ankles, then knees, then waist.

"Shuffle your feet," the woman ordered. "That way you don't surprise nothing, and nothing surprise you."

Priscilla did, moving slowly, moving carefully.

"Try floating," she advised. "Lay back. Now push your bottom up. Relax. Relax." Water lapped around and into Priscilla's ears. It held her up. The sky began to open, showing its stars. She did not know how long she bobbed.

When she went to stand, the sand would not meet her. Her feet went down, and down, and down, and nothing. She splashed, fighting for the surface, and the water fought back. Choked, water now inside her, kicking, breath pulling, pulling.

"Hey, hey, take it easy." Hands grabbing her arms. The woman was strong—superhuman, too strong. "Relax before you bring all three a us down." She could feel the woman's feet moving through the sea, treading water for them both. "You know where this is? This a blue hole. Just the tip of it. Just the start. This one go down a thousand feet. Six thousand, some people say. You believe that? The further down you go, the fresher the water is. Fresh, in the middle of the sea. So fresh you could drink. And deep, deep."

Priscilla's heart was still racing. "Deep like a mountain high?"

"Sure." The woman spoke smooth. "Deep like that."

Priscilla let go of the last bit of fight. As she did, the water stopped resisting her. "It's okay," the woman said. "I got you, it's okay."

"I arrite," Priscilla said. She heard the woman breathing, then not. In her head, *I'm okay. I'm okay.* She did not feel hands taking her to the shore. She felt the sandflies around her, tiny and invisible, aroused by the salt and night air.

∞

The house was dark as Priscilla drew close. Was Bible Study still going? She stepped up the stairs.

"What wrong with you?" Grammy burst out of the house, sudden, frenzied, a moth furious for fire. "Gone an break up the woman radio? You got money to buy things back, eh? You got money to pay for that? Where you been?" The old woman's fingers were tight on the girl's arm.

"By the beach." Priscilla heard her own voice shudder. Her legs felt like they were still in the water.

"Beach in the nighttime? Lord Jesus, help this girl, Lord, this girl possess. Devil get her, she possess, she possess. And she throw your Holy Word, use your book as a weapon, oh, Lord." Priscilla tried to pull her arm away but Grammy's nails dug in, her other hand waving the worn leather Bible. "Oh, Father, forgive her for she know not, she only a ignorant forceripe girl, God don' strike the girl down, oh, Lord."

"Grammy, my arm, you hurtin' me," she said, scrambling away, but the woman's hands came down heavily and shoved her to the ground. "Get out, Satan! Get out!" The old woman shook her granddaughter by the shoulders. Priscilla reached for the front door, pulling herself up. "Oh, Lord, forgive her," Grammy moaned into the air. She pulled the girl to her, praying and crying, and shoved her down again. Priscilla curled herself up, arms around her small belly.

"Mummy, stop it! Just stop!"

And there, suddenly, was the woman, out in the open, before her eyes, unanchored by beach or dock. Tall and proud-backed, dark eyes glistening. Grammy's face— shocked, cowed—and then Grammy seemed to melt away. The woman rushed to Priscilla and curled her hands over the girl's shoulders, then passed them across her midsection. Inside Priscilla, the baby lay still.

"You pass any blood? Get up, let me look," the woman said. She pulled Priscilla to her feet. Nothing. Priscilla closed her eyes, dark in dark. The voice came alto, earthy like sweet potato flesh. The woman covered Priscilla's stomach with her hands. Saying something. Something inside Priscilla turned and kicked. Once. She let herself be helped up onto the porch, guided into a chair.

"Call the nurse."

"She's coming." Grammy's voice shook. "Let the girl come inside. I'll wait with her."

"You think I'll leave her with you?"

"What you doin' here?" When Grammy spoke again, her strength was back. "Who send you here to come disruptin' people Christian household?"

The woman narrowed her eyes and adjusted the thin scarf at her throat. "That's how you's greet ya chirren now?"

Grammy glowered. "That's how you speak to your ma?"

"You claiming me now? This ain' even the time. How you do the girl like that? She pregnant."

Grammy turned away. "She fine. Think I don't know bout totin' baby? Forget who bring you and your sisters in this world?"

"I remember plenty. How to count. I remember Auntie Bessa-Mae's birthday fall six months after your anniversary. Same year too."

The front door creaked open.

"Esther, stop."

Grammy's hushed voice still reached Priscilla. Aunt Esther. She willed herself to follow their conversation, to focus on something other than her quiet belly.

"Come inside," Grammy pleaded.

"You really care what people hear? Everybody know. Secrets don't keep forever."

"Enough shame here already."

"Whose shame it is?" The woman's voice dropped then, and Priscilla had to strain to hear. "If you ain' wan' her, send her back with me tomorrow."

Grammy's reply was too quiet for Priscilla's ears, a faint ringing drowned her out.

In the street, someone passed, called out a greeting. "Mudda, that's ya last one there, eh? I ain' seen her in years."

Grammy didn't reply and the passerby carried on.

When Esther spoke again, her voice was twilight low. "Somebody ought to treat her right."

∞

Priscilla took the morning light in through her unswollen eye, let her body sink down onto the sea wall. The sun hit her body strong. She reached up to touch her face and winced. Inside her, nothing moved. *Strong heartbeat*, the nurse had said, the stethoscope cold against Priscilla's skin. *Strong heartbeat*, Priscilla told herself.

"Ain' I tell you stay inside today?" Her grandmother's voice cracked like a dry twig. "You cause enough trouble out here already." Priscilla turned. Behind the old woman, she thought she saw the church wall Jesus, slender and empty-handed, skin like sand and eyes water-blue. Grammy's black eyes glistened. Rotting fruit, guavas and something Priscilla couldn't name.

Grammy reached into the tangle of green, hesitated a moment, then snapped off a switch. "I'll take you down to the church if is the last thing I do. Lord, cast out this demon of blasphemy from this child, Lord, you know she carry enough sin already."

Priscilla stood and took a step back.

"Come now. Pastor Mason waitin', he ga pray for you."

Priscilla stumbled and Grammy caught her by both arms. Her grip softened as she guided the girl's slight limbs. She let the switch fall to the ground. She was only a child.

BOYO

DENISE WORRIED FOR HER CHILDREN in this new
land. Worried for Angie's tongue, which the girl had pierced
their seventh day here, as if marking a new Sabbath. It was
not so much the piercing—she knew Angie had done it
only for looks, for fun—but the way her daughter was
losing her words, trading them in for strange new ways of
speaking. Suddenly, she requested scones (pronounced
skohns, in a clipped, abbreviated style), complained about
the state of the "washroom" and delivered her sentences
with an accommodating upwards lilt, as though there was
uncertainty about the most certain of statements. "I hate
Science. And my mom doesn't even know I'm dropping it?"
Denise had heard her query into her phone. She fretted
for Calvin too, though this was not entirely new. He

seldom laughed, and hunkered into stacks of science books of his own choosing, with university-level studiousness.

And then there was Boyo. Boyo escaped out into the increasingly cold air at every opportunity, immersing himself in the outdoors as though, before coming to Canada, he'd been locked in a windowless four-by-four cell. Their first week in Vancouver he had liberated himself by standing on a chair and unlocking the chain on the front door. They installed a second lock, trickier and higher up, one an eight-year-old should not have been able to reach. No matter. The second week, Denise had woken chilled through and came to the top of the stairs to see the front door swinging wide. The other children slept obediently in their beds; Boyo's sheets were thrown back, the mattress cold. The side table had been pushed by the front door, her new orchid teetering on the edge, three phone books propped up beside the plant, rumpled by small feet.

She found him on the sidewalk out front, crouched beside the grass verge between walkway and street. A fine rain fell. When she called to him, her voice a net thrown out over her boy, he looked up, eyes shining.

"Mummy, look!" He pointed down. A row of earthworms stretched across the width of the wet sidewalk, their back ends still burrowed into the bordering soil. He could not understand her anger as she pulled him up the stairs and back inside.

∞

Calvin, at least, she could love right. In the bathroom, after she'd cleaned behind his ears with a damp washcloth, she would move in close to press her face against the tight bulb of his cheek.

"Mummy, what are you doing?" he would ask, and she would be embarrassed.

"I'm checking your skin."

"Mummy, stop sniffing my hair."

Busted, she would recommence rinsing the soap off his smooth baby skin while he recounted, with zest, the contents of *The Incredible World of Science* or whatever his book of the day happened to be.

∞

In the mornings, when the children had gone to school and Amos had gone to work, she wandered the aisles of Superstore. They stocked nearly everything she needed: oil, flour, several types of vegetables, even the occasional mango, promisingly yellow if utterly infragrant. One thing eluded her: she could not find cassava.

"I think they call it yucca?" Angie said over dinner, one eyebrow cocked as though Denise really ought to be better educated. She ignored the girl.

"I been all up and down the food store, asking where they keep the cassava. The manager look at me like I was crazy, and finally say he would make a note of it and if enough people ask for it, they might bring it in."

"Did you ask for yucca?"

"So I thought we could each go in separately and ask. Five people asking, that's a start, right?"

"Just ask for yucca! Geez."

Denise's fork clattered as it hit her plate. "What you say?"

"Geez," Calvin parroted dutifully.

"I think the Cubans call it yucca, they might know it by that name here," Amos said, pushing his chair back.

"It could be with a G . . . or a J?"

"G." Amos lifted his plate. "And a Z at the end."

"What did you say?" she asked Angie again. "Did you just sit here and swear?"

"*Geez* isn't a swear?" Her black-rimmed eyes were defiant.

"'Geez,'" Calvin announced, head bent over his trusty little dictionary. "'A eeww—eewppp . . .'"

Denise leaned over to look at the page. "Euphemism."

"What's that?"

"Why don't you look that up too, genius?" Angie snipped.

"Leave your brother alone." Denise tried to keep her voice even. "A euphemism is a nicer way of saying something. And no books at the table during dinner, Cal."

"'A euphemism for Jesus.'"

Angie scowled at the boy. "Like anybody asked you?"

Denise picked her fork up again. "Watch your mouth."

"What's the big deal?" Angie muttered into her plate.

"'Used,'" Calvin continued triumphantly, "'as a swear or minor oath.'"

"That's enough, Calvin." Amos plucked the dictionary from Calvin's hands and snapped it shut. "Eat your dinner."

"Thou shalt not take the Lord Thy God's name in vain," the boy added, shovelling green peas into his mouth.

Angie made a face at him. "Mind your own business, four-eyes."

"I don't wear glasses."

Denise watched the two children, oldest and youngest, with the sense of observing a goldfish and a guppy through thick glass and slightly dirty water as they circled each other. She should, she knew, intervene, should snap at one to stop egging on the other. She turned, instead, to look at Boyo. He was chewing slowly, his face tilted toward the window.

He must have felt her gaze. He turned to look at her, still chewing. "Mummy, I could be excused?"

She reached over, running a hand over the satisfying roundness of his head. "Finish your dinner first, Boyo."

"I don't wear glasses!" Calvin said again.

Angie leaned toward the younger boy. "Bring your face here, I could fix that."

Denise pushed her plate away. Amos got up.

"Just watch your mouth, girl." Amos' voice brought an end to the bickering; the two children sank into silence, one sullen, the other smug.

Denise rose from the table and began collecting the empty dishes. She turned to whisper to Amos that he shouldn't play favourites, shouldn't assume Calvin was right and Angie wrong, but he was already gone. She reached over and picked up Calvin's plate. Beside him, Boyo's chair was also suddenly empty.

"Where's your brother?"

"Outside." Angie's chair was already pushed out before she added, "Can I go now?"

∞

After Denise found Boyo two blocks down, squatting by a tree stump, inspecting the spot where a skunk had just vanished with a quick flash of its white tail, she and Amos had the talk with him again. That he had to stay put. That someone might hurt him. Someone might take him. He had to be careful here.

"Why somebody would do that?"

"You never heard of pedophiles, eh?" Angie had wandered into the kitchen, as if divinely attuned to the opportunity to disrupt and disturb.

"What's a pedophile?" Boyo's eyes turned to Denise. Angie smirked as she opened the refrigerator door. Denise opened her mouth, hoping an answer would follow. But Boyo was already up by the window again, threat forgotten, nose pressed to the pane. "Look, Mummy, a dog. We could go see?" He turned to look at her, eyes pleading, then turned back to watch outside, the fog of his breath fanning out over the glass.

∞

Denise answered the phone on the second ring. "Hello?" she said, dripping errant tub water and soap. Though the air was brisk, she felt flushed with guilty warmth to be caught soaking mid-morning on a weekday. She added, "Denise Symonette speaking," because she suddenly thought it might be a call about her work visa. She tightened the towel around her chest.

"Yes, hello, this is Kelly from Bay Drive Elementary calling. Is this William's mother?"

"Boyo?" Her voice came out in a spasm, a gasp. "This is William's mother, yes," she corrected herself. "Is everything okay?"

∞

She recognized the back of his round head through the office window, still mostly bare from his Back to School clean-shave. She pulled him to her, then cuffed the side of his head. "What wrong with you, though? You stupid, eh?"

He scrunched up his nose, looking away from her, and rubbed his head with one hand.

"The principal will be out in a minute," the receptionist said. Denise nodded.

Denise sat beside Boyo on a chair too small for her behind. "What, Boyo? What's wrong with you? You're almost nine. You don't know better than to run away from school?"

Boyo shrugged.

"Yes, you know. What? What would make you do something so silly?"

He murmured something he did not want her to hear.

"What's that?"

"I was just looking."

"Looking? Boyo . . ." She lowered her voice. "Did you peek at a girl?"

"I ain' know if it was a girl, I was just looking. Mummy, how you know if a squirrel is a boy or a girl?"

The principal's door opened suddenly, mercifully. The principal—a woman, short, thin, greying—nodded at her briskly. "You must be William's mother."

"Denise Symonette."

"Come on in, Mrs. Symonette. You can stay right there on the chair, William—thank you."

Boyo scowled, squirming slightly. She disliked this

woman's firm way of speaking to her boy, and disliked, even more, his sudden obedience.

"Maybe he should come in—" she began.

"It's okay. The receptionist will make sure he doesn't disappear again."

"Don't move." Denise gathered her handbag to her. "I mean it."

"We found him," the principal explained in her office, once Denise had closed the door behind herself, "after he wandered off in the middle of class time. He was completely safe, but I have to tell you, we're concerned. This is the third time he's left class."

"Where was he?"

"We found him across the road from the school—as you know, there's a fair bit of traffic along this street, too. He was behind some shrubs."

In the bush, Denise thought. *Figures my child would have to go stick himself in some stupid place.*

"We're concerned by William's behaviour, Mrs. Symonette." The principal reached into a drawer. "I'd like to give you some reading material."

Denise extended her hand automatically. *Parenting the Troubled Child. After Immigration: Helping Your Child Adjust.* "Thank you," she said. Her voice felt thick and foreign.

Walking out into the schoolyard, Denise fumed. Something wrong with her child. Concerned. *The receptionist will make sure,* the woman had said, as though Denise somehow would not.

"Stay here with me." Denise's grip on Boyo's wrist tightened as she bent down to look him in the eye. "Boyo, you can't keep doing this."

"Mummy, you hurting me." He squirmed, his face twisting in dramatized agony. Breaking free from her, he dropped his bag and books, running to chase after a dumpy brown bird that, at his footsteps, took flight. As Denise ran after him, she expected, for a moment, that Boyo would spread his arms wide and rise into the air, while her feet remained heavily, sensibly, pulled down.

∞

That afternoon, Angie came inside with Calvin after school; usually the girl deposited the boys at home, then disappeared. The library, she claimed, or the coffee shop. She never clarified which coffee shop—there were six or seven in the neighbourhood.

"How was school?" Denise asked from the dining table. The girl shrugged. Denise braced herself for a snide comment about Boyo's truancy.

"You did laundry?" Angie said instead.

Denise looked up from the computer. "You want clean clothes, you know how to operate the washer and dryer. And toss the boys' clothes in there too." She tensed for a battle. She was tired of fighting this pierced, choppy-haired girl, her face made new every day with colours that seemed not to exist anywhere else.

Angie didn't answer, instead she leaned in over Denise's shoulder, squinting at the screen. The focus on her face, brow furrowed, chin slightly raised, was so like Denise's own mother that it nearly took her breath away.

"Immigration Canada?"

Denise snapped the laptop closed. "I was checking my application status."

"What happened? I thought our visas were good for three years." Under the new lilt in Angie's voice, Denise could detect the faintest tremor.

"They are, everything's fine," Denise answered quickly. "I just applied for a work permit. Just to—"

"I get it." Angie straightened up. "I can wash. Want me to do yours and Daddy's clothes too?"

Denise felt a smile threatening to emerge as she raised her eyes to Angie's. "If you like."

∞

The next time the school called, she was in the library. She answered the phone stealthily, afraid someone might kiss their teeth at her. And the next, she was in the produce aisle. "Yucca," she was saying, measuring out the length of a cassava root with her hands, nine inches, a foot. "Brown, the skin's waxed, inside is white. You eat it like potato. You know, yucca!" The store clerk, who evidently did not know, seemed relieved when Denise's phone rang, and escaped hastily. The time after that, she was on hold with Immigration's call centre, nine minutes into her wait, torn between staying on the line and running out the door to go into the small office in person and accept a fresh stack of brochures and judgment.

∞

At night, she went in to look at the children sleeping. She had to do this late; Angie had taken to staying up past eleven, claiming homework, but while her nose might be in a book, her headphones were always attached to her phone. Even asleep, the girl's earbuds were in. Denise reached down to remove them. *She must be recharging the battery that powers her sarcasm*, Denise thought as she shut the phone down and put it on the nightstand. The girl twisted away, grumbling in her sleep, her long limbs like stretched toffee.

Calvin lay in a line down the centre of his bed as if feigning sleep, arms at his sides under the blankets, legs straight and stiff. Only his small bow mouth was relaxed, open like a secret half-told. His nose twitched when she kissed his forehead.

At Boyo's bed, she whispered to his small body, sprawled diagonally across the mattress or buried under pillows and duvets. "Why you doing it, baby?" she asked. "What you seeing out there? Why you running away?"

∞

Weekends, she took them all on walks. "Calvin," she heard herself say, "get your gumboots on." *Gumboots*. The word felt chewy and slick, a gelatinous candy worm removed from a damp mouth. She wanted to say *galoshes* like in the old English stories her mother had read to her as a girl. "Angie, you coming?"

"Um, yeah?" The girl's voice rang out sharp from her bedroom.

From the kitchen window, Denise watched Boyo on the lawn, dancing in the way little boys do before they learn otherwise. He grabbed handfuls of leaves, tossing brown fistfuls into the air. Angie appeared in the kitchen. Her eyes were rimmed with an electric blue that jangled against her dark skin, her lips dipped in red. Her eyes passed over the scene outside, heavy with judgment and clumpy mascara.

"I hope you know dogs pissed all over those leaves." She rammed her feet into athletic shoes. Calvin's gumboots were on now, his jacket halfway zipped.

"Watch your mouth." Denise rummaged through her bag, hunting for her wallet.

"What? *Pissed* isn't a curse."

"It's in the Bible," Calvin volunteered. "Remember, the minister said it one time when we were in Nassau . . . Something about men that pisseth against—"

"Peed! Just say peed, okay?" Denise wished, as soon as she had spoken, that she had not snapped. "You wanna help your brother with his coat?" she added, trying to keep her voice level.

"What you wearing boots for, it ain't even raining." Angie's earbuds were in again. Of course.

"I like them." Calvin yanked away from her, tugging at the zipper himself. Outside, leaves rose in puffs, then scattered as they fell.

∞

The park stretched out before them. Wild grass, yellowed and dried, lined the gravel path; low creeks snaked alongside the walkways, disappeared into the growth, then resurfaced later, petering into marshland. East, the ocean was a deep, strange blue. Boyo moved like four or five different boys, now stealthy, now slow and quiet, now quick and light, slipping between shadows, checking the path for crossing caterpillars, clumsy black-and-red things heavy with fur. When he found one, he would block the path from feet and bicycle tires until it had completed its passage. In a pinch, he would scoop it up and deposit it on the grass.

"You're messing with nature, you know," Angie observed from under her halo of music.

"No, I'm not."

"Yeah, if they too slow, they haven't adapted, and it's nature's way of weeding them out."

"I don't want anyone to step on them."

"It's called natural selection, worm boy."

"I ain't no worm."

Calvin was engrossed in a book, his legs maintaining reluctant motion as he trailed behind.

"What's this you reading?" Denise asked, squatting down to his eye level.

"*Harry Potter.*" Calvin didn't look up.

"Isn't that a bit old for you?"

"The librarian said I might like it. And Angie read it ages ago, Mom."

"*Mom?*" She reeled back from the word. "What happen to *Mummy?*"

Calvin shot her a look of disgust and turned his eyes back down to the page. Denise snatched the book away from him.

"Hey!" he said. "Mom, I could have my book back? Please, Mummy?"

Denise stuffed the novel into her purse. "Enjoy nature. Be a boy. What wrong with you?" She picked up the pace. "Come on, see the others getting ahead?"

Calvin was shuffling now, his feet moving so slowly he was almost standing still. She gritted her teeth and pulled the book out again, shoved it toward the boy. He brightened, snatching it, and trotted along beside her. They were almost caught up to Angie and Boyo now.

"Look, Boyo, you missed one," Angie said, pointing the tip of her red nail at a caterpillar that lay across the path, unmoving. "It's okay," she said, "I'll help."

Her foot descended before Boyo's fingers could reach the caterpillar. It made a crunch that gave way to a squelch.

"No!" He darted away down the path, his face twisted with anger and sorrow.

Angie lifted her foot. "It was already dead anyway."

"When did you become such a bitch?" The words tumbled out of Denise's mouth before she could stop them. The girl flinched, as if she had been slapped. "Angie, I—" But then she stopped. The earbuds were back in, music back on, and her apology wouldn't be heard.

"Bitch . . . bitch . . ." Calvin murmured, and then Denise heard the flutter of his pocket dictionary's pages. Boyo was almost out of sight.

"Hey, slow down," she called ahead, knowing her voice couldn't carry. "Walk up," she chided Calvin, who had closed his dictionary now, apparently uninterested in sharing the definition of this particular new word with the parkgoers around them. "Go find your brother."

Bitch. The word loomed in her mind. She straightened up, scanning the grassy area around them. Boyo's red jacket flashed through the overgrowth. She let out a long breath she hadn't known she'd been holding. Relief, then a flicker of anger. "See him there?" she said to Calvin. "Go on, go play with your brother."

"But he's not supposed to be in there. It says *Please Keep On The Path*."

"You're only young once. Live a little." Strained clichés tumbled from her lips.

"It says it right back there." Calvin pointed just over Denise's shoulder.

"Just go!"

"You better listen, you don't want her throwing slurs at you too." Angie didn't look their way, but she'd stopped walking, staring down the path, hands deep in her pockets.

Denise tried to remember back to when she was four-teen. Her own mother, sullen and plump, glaring at her from supermarket aisles as she tried to sneak a word or two to the cute stock boy, and picking up the kitchen phone while Denise whispered into the living room line about whoever she had a crush on that week. This was how it had to be, then.

And then Boyo was bounding up to her, his hands cupped one over the other. "Look what I found." He lifted the left one for a moment. A grasshopper, still as dry sticks, waited in his palm, poised to escape. He closed his hand over it again like a dungeon door. Denise smiled.

"That's nice, Boyo. Why you don't go show your sister?"

∞

In the evening, after dinner, Amos made them write letters home.

Angie rolled her eyes. "Why don't we just crawl back into the 1800s?"

"Your grandmother says she misses getting letters, so y'all ga write letters."

He lined them up at the table, each with regulation 8½" x 11" ruled paper and fine-tipped blue pens. Denise absented herself, clattering dishes in the sink with one hand to disguise the sound of wine pouring into a glass.

"I don't see why we can't just send an email."

Amos ignored the observation, moving into the living room, turning on the news.

Boyo fidgeted in his seat. "How come Mummy ain't writing?"

"Mummy wrote hers already," Denise said from the kitchen. She could feel the wine becoming a part of her, her body beginning to tinge with plumminess, light-headed, thick-hipped. She took another sip, then began to stack the rinsed plates into the dishwasher.

"Mummy? How you spell *alonely*?" Boyo called.

"*Alonely* ain't no word, dummy," Angie said.

"Mummy?" Boyo said again.

"Yes, baby?" Her legs were turning to thick liquid, but the word tightened something in her. "What's this about *alonely*? You mean *alone*? Or *lonely*?"

"Both." Boyo scratched his head. Such a sweet, obvious move—a thinking boy *should* scratch his head.

"A-l-o-n-e-l-y," she said, setting her glass down.

"Daddy, Boyo making up words," Calvin said.

"Let's not bother Daddy. What you writing to Grammy? Hey?" Denise stepped into the dining room, leaned over and scanned Calvin's paper.

Dear Grammy,
Daddy said to write a letter to you. Canada is fine. We live in a place called Vancouver. I would rather read my book, but Daddy is making us write to you.

"I'm not finished." Calvin leaned over the letter, covering it with his crooked arm. Denise looked over Angie's letter. The writing was too small for her to read it, but the page was almost full. "You think Grammy's eyes could take that?"

"She only writing about *Jacob*," Calvin said.

"Her boyfriend." Boyo sounded eager to clarify.

"Y'all shut your big mouths." Angie turned up the volume on her earphones.

"If I can hear your music over the TV, it's *too loud*," Amos called.

"Can I do this in my room?" Angie said.

Denise looked into the girl's face. Her eyes were outlined with dark green now, her mouth shimmery and gold.

Denise would never have dared to wear so much makeup in her mother's house. She would probably never dare to wear so much makeup now. "G'on, then."

The words were barely spoken before Angie was thundering up the stairs.

"Hey!" Amos said, almost in a shout, before catching himself. "*Softly.*"

"*Alonely* isn't a real word," Calvin said, peering up from his open dictionary.

"Live longer." Denise's voice came out louder than she meant it to. "I just mean you'll understand, in time," she said. Calvin didn't answer. She heard herself giggle then, silly and high.

∞

On the Tuesday when his face turned up at the kitchen window just before ten, she nearly cut herself peeling onions. She opened the kitchen door and he scurried inside, eager, for once, to enter the house.

"Boyo! Why you ain't in school?"

He opened his hand. In it was curled a small, thick-bodied spider. "Could I keep it?"

She started, then folded his fingers back over the thing and urged him toward the door. "Outside." She stood and watched, onion hanging loose in her hand, while he gently brushed his palm against a bush, whispering.

"You come all the way home for this?" she scolded. "Who told you to leave school?" But she let him stay, calling the office from the backyard. The principal listened while Denise prattled that Boyo was fine, that he had come home to show her a spider he had found, that she would talk to him, that it wouldn't happen again. When her words trailed off, a thick silence settled between them. Finally, the principal cleared her throat.

"Since this is"—papers rustled on the other end—"the ninth time William has run off during the school day, I'm afraid we'll be placing him on a two-week suspension."

"But—"

"Mrs. Symonette, this has gone on too long. William has exceeded his additional chances." Denise almost welcomed the interruption; she had not known how to protest any more.

"I'll see that he thinks about his actions," Denise said.

"When I say he has exceeded his chances," the principal continued, as though Denise had not spoken, "I mean that he may not be the best fit for this school." Her voice was quiet. "We won't stop him from returning, and he will continue to have a place here, but . . ."

Denise hung up. She did not need to hear what the principal would say next. She texted Angie to let her know only Calvin would be walking home with her after school, and caught a glimpse of her reflection in the window, phone in one hand, onion still in the other.

How come he gets to skip school and I have to be here all day?
Angie texted back. Denise had no answer. She let the phone
slip out of her fingers and onto the ground. She sat down
next to it, tossing the onion from hand to hand, watching
as Boyo chased some invisible thing through the grass.

∞

The brown government envelope arrived three days into
Boyo's suspension. She glanced out the window. Boyo,
hunched down in a squat, peering up into the body of a
tree. "Stay off the street," she shouted, her voice held cap-
tive by the closed windows.

Dear Denise Symonette,
This letter is in reference to your application for a Canadian
work permit. After careful review, we have determined
that your application does not meet the requirements . . .

She balled the letter up and flung it into the garbage.
Her throat felt thick, full, as though hot tears were welling
up there. She could already hear Amos' response. *You don't*
need to work, you know. I make enough. As though his abun-
dance of money gave her life meaning.

"Mummy?" Boyo in the doorway.

He held something. Flat and nearly big as his head,
patchily red and ripe orange and almost-there yellow,

like mango skin. She wiped her damp face. He extended his hand to her.

"Bring it here."

It was a leaf, she could see that now. Five-pronged, still supple, still alive.

"You want it?" His face was concerned. "You take it, Mummy, you take the leaf."

"Thank you, Boyo." She wrapped her arms around him. She was vaguely aware that her embrace was too tight; he squirmed, and she let him go.

"Mummy—you okay?"

"Yes, Boyo." She twirled his present by its stem. "That's nice. I'm gonna put this on my nightstand. G'on, go play outside again, okay?"

Alone, Denise removed the letter from the garbage. The bag had been fresh, the letter had shared space only with a paper towel she had used to shine the window panes. She straightened it out, folded it in half, pressed the leaf in between, and put it in the drawer, beneath her passport.

∞

The day Boyo's suspension was up, she walked with her two youngest to school. Angie had taken a different route, waiting outside their house for a pair of friends—a tall girl, her hair reedy and black, the other plump and redheaded with extraordinarily large breasts, obvious beneath her thin sweatshirt. The girls huddled, breath rising in the dusky morning air.

Calvin's hands were rammed into the pockets of his jacket. In his black wool button-up, he was a six-year-old miniature of Amos.

"Don't you like this one better?" she had said, shopping for jackets their second day here, pointing out a nice blue one emblazoned with Superman on the back.

"Mummy, that's *so* not him," Angie had said. Calvin, silent, had edged a step closer to his sister. Denise had been mildly irritated at the time. Now, she glanced over at him, trudging along, the smallest shoulder bag they could find tucked sideways over his body—*God help him when he hits his teens*, she thought. *Or will the teasing start before that? Has it already begun?*

"Boyo!" He had run ahead, and had now disappeared behind someone's shrubbery. "These people ga think I raising a little vagabond. Boyo, come back here."

He emerged from around the bushes, a large, smooth stone in one hand. It was one of the beachside rocks people seemed to like to use for decoration here. In August, when they had arrived in Vancouver, the rocks had been dull and dusty lumps, but as the weather dampened, they changed into smooth, slick things that winked in the tepid daylight. Boyo waited for them to catch up to him, half obeying Denise's order.

"You put that back. Go on, put it back in their yard. That's stealing."

"But it's a rock," he protested.

"And that's their tree, you want to dig that up, too?"

Boyo made that face of displeasure common to boys receiving illogical instructions. He finally dropped the rock, letting it clatter onto its comrades below.

"Listen," she told him, "now, I don't want any trouble from you. You stay in the classroom, you stay with your teacher, you don't go sneaking out."

Boyo fidgeted. "But it's boring."

Great preparation for adulthood, she thought. "Never mind," she said instead. His eyes had drifted over to a pair of small birds flitting about. They were a dull grey-brown, and made high, clicking noises to each other.

"It ain't no fair."

"You know what, Boyo, we all have jobs we have to do. Daddy's job is to go to the office, or to go on a trip, even if he's tired. Your teacher's job is to come to school and put up with all of you wriggling in your seats and talking to your friends when you're supposed to be quiet."

Boyo grimaced.

"And give you homework that she has to mark at night, even if she'd rather go out dancing." They were at the school now, just outside Boyo's classroom. Through the window, she could see his teacher straightening the already tidy desks, mothlike in a grey and beige blouse and pants.

"Teachers don't go out dancing," Calvin cut in.

Boyo laughed. "Especially not Miss Warner."

"But maybe she'd like to. Maybe she'd rather spend the whole day on the swings instead of teaching you multiplication tables."

"We don't do multiplication tables here. Miss Warner say that's old-fashioned."

"Well, whatever. Maybe Miss Warner would rather be stuffing her face with ice cream and beer and getting silly and falling all over the floor!" Her voice rose to a giddy pitch. She began to tickle him. Boyo pushed her away, giggling. Then he yielded, allowing her to hold him close for a moment, like she had when he was much smaller.

"Mummy, what's your job?"

If the question had come from Angie, she would have bristled. Instead, she carried on silently toward the school's entrance, aware of the four small ears waiting patiently for her answer.

"My job is to take care of you. Gone, now, go inside."

He hugged her tighter.

"If you can get through the whole week of school without running away, on the next sunny day, I'll take us all to the park again."

She stayed by the doors after they had gone in, then backtracked, pausing by the window they'd passed together minutes earlier. Through the glass, she saw the students settling at their desks, Boyo too, in his space near the front of the room. Somewhere, through an open door or window, a teacher's voice floated out, singsongy and high, sure of herself. Denise stayed until someone stopped and said, "Can I help you?" with an irritated smile, and she shook herself loose and carried on.

∞

Saturday came, bringing rare sun. Amos was working, again. Angie had gone off with friends, so Denise began rounding up her sons for the walk she had promised Boyo in exchange for good behaviour. She felt lighter, even hopeful. Boyo was exuberant, ready to go before he had properly washed and eaten, Calvin slow to remove himself from the computer.

"What are you doing on there?" She peered at the screen. The electronic encyclopedia they had bought for him was up.

"I'm looking at the entry on The Bahamas," Calvin said. She leaned over his shoulder. It was strange to see their entire country summed up in three short paragraphs wrapped around a picture of a beach resort.

"You miss home?"

Calvin leaned back from the screen. "It's just research."

At the park, the air was strange. Standing still, in the sun, it was almost warm, but the shadows had soaked up frigid air and breathed it out, sharp, straight through to their bones. Even so, Boyo seemed at home. Denise watched him disappear into hollows, slipping beneath the thorny archways of blackberry bushes in search of birds, then emerging from the stalks of overgrown marsh plants.

"Stay on the path," Calvin complained, looking up from his book from time to time.

She and Calvin found a place on a bench in the sun and sat down. "Don't go too far," she called, her voice carrying only halfway to Boyo. She closed her eyes for a moment, letting the sun saturate her. Like this, she could almost be out on Cabbage Beach—the salty tang to the air, the sunshine, the quiet. It was almost like she fit in. Like she was home. A seagull, somewhere off to the right, gave its warning call.

She snapped her eyes open, automatically searching for Boyo. All she could see was the scrubby brush, sky and ocean far beyond. "You see your brother?"

"He's over there." Calvin didn't look up, only pointed in the general direction of where the sun would set. High weeds, dry and gold. Boyo was standing on the sloped bank of an inlet. Below him, the water was perfect, still.

"Boyo! Boyo, come, you gone too far. Remember, you're to stay on the path."

He turned and waved, his face invisible, silhouetted by the sun. Then he fell. The splash was thick. His body went down into the water, his shout lifting into the air.

"Boyo!" She ran toward him, ran and ran. People gathering already, a man, two, four, shoving past her. Boyo's head surfacing, then dipping under, panicked splashing, arms frantic, working, and that water, thick and brown. Someone said *It's slippery!* and pulled her back as she lunged for Boyo. She thrashed free, but already he was out of the dark water, the men pulling him up by his flailing limbs, *Settle down, son, settle down, it's all right now.* Coughing, crying and shivering, a siren's wail drawing near, certain to arrive before she could reach him.

∞

They ate dinner in silence while, upstairs, Boyo slept.

"I don't want y'all going to that park again. Ever." Amos glared at Boyo's empty chair. "And when he wakes up in the morning, boy, I ga have some words for him. I knew his running off would get him in trouble."

Denise set her fork down hard. "No, you won't."

Angie pushed her chair back.

"Where are you going?" Amos asked.

"May I be excused?"

"Go on." She and Amos answered at the same time.

"Where are you going?" he repeated.

"To the coffee shop."

"Tonight?" Denise heard her own voice crack.

"Not like I'm gonna go falling into some ditch."

"Talk to your mother like that? Get out this house," Amos snapped.

"Be back by nine," Denise called after her, but her words were caught in the slamming door. It enraged her, what this child could do to her. She—*don't think it*—hated the girl.

∞

Later that night, Denise moved around the house, tucking in chairs, picking up discarded socks. In the bedroom, she wiped a day's worth of dust off the nightstand, then opened the drawer. Their passports lay, neatly stacked. Each was navy blue, the coat of arms etched in gold. What would her children do, if she got into the car, drove to the airport? If she just kept on going? How long would it be before each of them missed her?

"Can you watch Boyo?" she asked, downstairs. Amos glanced up from his papers.

"Sure."

She heard the tilt to his voice, that hint of disapproval. She was a bad mother. Far worse than Angie being a bad daughter—this was a trait Denise would not outgrow.

She took her keys and her bag, then stepped out into the autumn evening air. No trace of sun now. It had clouded over, thick and close. She walked down the sidewalk, avoiding the odd person on a bike, vaguely smiling at a woman pushing a stroller. *At this time of night*, she thought, then reminded herself that here she was, strolling after dark, while her son recovered at home, remembered his lungs filling with dirty creek water, the thrash of his helpless limbs.

Across the street was one of the six coffee shops in their neighbourhood. Outside, some feet away from the door, a cluster of young people had formed, white mist rising above their heads. She stopped, watching them. Even some of the girls smoked. She could not imagine doing such a thing. She searched for Angie's familiar shape, but from here, all the girls looked the same, slight variations in height, in weight, but each a similar blur of makeup, hoodie, leggings, flat fluffy boots, and she could not pick out her child.

∞

A wind picked up, though there were no clouds to clear away. She reached the park quickly, no one on the path before or behind her. At the spot where Boyo had fallen in, shoeprints still decorated the muddy earth, ovals ridged and cross-hatched. She squatted down. These small ones, and these, and these, were her son's. He must have been looking up, not straight ahead, watching some winged thing move quick through the brush, wishing to fly. She reached into her bag, and brought out Boyo's leaf, twirling it. She swept her arm up then, flicking her wrist, and set the leaf on the air. It danced against the hard sky, caught a gust and hovered a moment before it began to fall toward the water that would buoy it until it didn't.

She reached into her purse again, for the letter, and swung her arm once more, setting the paper free. The page landed flat. She watched, her fingers growing cold, as it drooped and slowly sank. She wondered how long it would be before the bleached sheet and black ink surrendered to their fate in the water's bed, how long before its strange parts would give in and become a part of this place.

THIN WATER

MANGO SUMMER

IT WAS A FRUITFUL SUMMER. People tend to forget that.

Everyone was giving dilly away. The boys sold guineps at all the big intersections, straight from their hands. Dollar for a big bunch, then fifty cents, then twenty-five. Too many guineps to waste money bagging them. The boys pocketed the quarters, then spent them on candy. No one made a profit. Sugar apples melted off trees and lay open on the ground, splattered buffets left for the rats. People were stacking up mangoes on the grass at the edges of their properties to be taken away, and leaving unmarked brown bags of sickly-ripe fruit on each other's doorsteps.

The air was slick with August humidity from the first week in May, and so tight with the smell it hazed orange. It did something to people. Abe Pratt, who used to beg bareback all morning and drink all afternoon, was so changed that by mid-July, he appeared (sober) at New Roots Baptist Church's revival week in reasonably clean pants, a crinkled blue shirt no one had known he owned, and hair trimmed so low everyone was surprised by how small his head was.

I was ten that summer. Theresa was eight. Both the perfect errand-running ages, small enough not to talk back too bad, big enough to carry boxes to and from Sweet Mouth, who we were supposed to call Miz Liza even though no one else did, not even Mummy when she forgot to be respectful herself or thought we weren't listening. The boxes went as fruit and came back as jam, twice as heavy. Theresa told Mummy this was because Sweet Mouth put ground-up rocks inside everything she made, and we shouldn't carry any more fruit to her to cook up. And plus, didn't we have enough mangoes around already? Couldn't we throw them away? Weren't there hungry children somewhere around who wanted them? We didn't need jam.

She had a point. The backyard's sweet reek leaked into the kitchen, and also the bathroom, because its window faced that side of the yard, so that it no longer smelled like soap or bleach or pee, as a bathroom should, but like rotting fruit salad. The freezer was crammed with mango purée.

We weren't the only people on Earth, Mummy reminded us. We didn't know what she was going to do with the jam. And why were we here talking? Too much talking, not enough work. Hurry up, take those boxes so Sweet—so Miz Liza could get them made up. And we better stay behind long enough to find out if she needed help peeling and dicing.

Theresa and I knew better. The jam would be with us every day for the next six years. All food would become a suspected carrier. It would cover our bread. It would sneak into our cookies, it would appear swirled into muffins, glaze-baked chicken, replace cheddar in the macaroni and cheese. It would be an integral part of our diets until Theresa or I got married, when Mummy would send us away with so many cases of mango jam there'd be no space in the new house for the husband.

Perhaps, we agreed, as we turned down Sweet Mouth's street, the filled jars would have an accident on the way back.

We got to Sweet Mouth's house just as Nay, my classmate from nine houses down, was leaving.

"Hey, Nay, you got cookies?" Theresa said.

Nay's wide-set eyes slid toward us, suspicious of my sister's intent. Sure enough, the girl had a small foil package tucked under one arm, and crumbs around her mouth— Theresa could pick out a parcel of goodies anywhere, particularly if it didn't have mango chunks in it. Nay said something that was probably meant to be "No," tightened her grip around her precious bundle with the earnest greed of a girl who had four brothers, slammed the gate shut and ran off. I set down my box so I could open the gate again, while Theresa stuck out her tongue at Nay's back.

At the door, Theresa dropped her burden. "Miz Sweet Mouth!" she hollered through the screen door, in a way that would have infuriated our mother. Nudging her with my elbow, I knocked politely on the wooden frame. Through the grey mesh, we could see the tiny woman washing a huge mound of plums at her sink.

"Brenda, that's hog plum she washin'?" Theresa asked. I was skeptical, too. No one washed hog plums in a sink. They were eaten outside. The seeds were spat out in the grass. They weren't even in season yet. No decent person had hog plums until late summer. It was May.

"Come in," Sweet Mouth called over the running water. Theresa opened the door, skipping in empty-handed. I followed, setting my box down on the floor. The kitchen was stickily hot and smelled of syrup.

"What you makin'?" Theresa asked, as Sweet Mouth poured the small green fruit into a large pot. I elbowed my sister again.

"Miz Liza, Mummy say bring these to you for jam," I announced.

"Hmph. How many that is? Two boxes?" She stirred at the improper plums. "Go look in the dining room, see if I have any empty jars for this jam y'all want me make."

"What you doin'?" Theresa was on tiptoe, practically climbing into the pot. Standing like that, she came up almost to the woman's shoulder.

"Boiling them for punch," Sweet Mouth said. She

glanced back at me. "Missy, you ain' gone yet for those jars? Look by the chairs, I have some clean ones in there somewhere."

Scowling, I retreated into her dingy inner sanctum. How come I had to do the scary stuff? Theresa was the one always sticking her nose into things when she shouldn't, I thought, then scolded myself. I was older. I should be responsible.

"An your ma pregnant again?" Sweet Mouth was asking in the kitchen. I hoped Theresa wouldn't say anything dumb. My eyes darted around the dim room. Dog-eared phone book on the dining table. Dusty vase with four plastic flowers, petals thick and waxy-red. A white brocade sofa covered in plastic, even though she had no children. It looked like no one had ever sat on it. I wondered if she was saving the sofa for something. On the floor next to it, in paper bags, were four huge plastic jars.

"New baby in October," I heard Theresa saying. I grabbed up the jars and turned back to the kitchen before Theresa blabbed out all our family business.

"These?" I held the containers toward Sweet Mouth.

"Glass, girl, glass. You know what happen if you put hot jam inside plastic? Go look again. I need to send your baby sister to help you look?"

In the dining room, I peered under the table, then jumped back. A huge spiderweb was woven from the wall to the table leg closest to me. The only other thing there was brown paper bags full of sugar packets. The owner of the dusty web skittered as I dropped the tablecloth. I looked over the top of the table again, then at the spot where I'd found the plastic jars. Finally, my eyes lit upon a closed box on the chair that stood by the table, its back pressed awkwardly against the wall. I gingerly opened the lid, and the rims of twelve jars winked out at me. I lifted the box carefully.

". . . like little girls," Sweet Mouth was saying into the pot, as I came back in. "Took you long enough," she said, her back to me. "Put them on the counter."

Theresa was draining the last of something from a little pink cup.

"Y'all go, leave me, let me do my work."

I dragged Theresa out. When we were a few houses away, I cuffed her in the back of her head. "You stupid, eh? What you was drinkin'?"

"Coconut water." Theresa rubbed her head, glaring at me. "You just jealous you ain' get none."

"You too greedy." We walked on another few minutes before I asked, "What she said about girls?"

"I ain' tellin you."

I knew I'd get it out of her. She wouldn't stay mad long. She'd tell me that night, when we stretched out in bed, hoisting the sheet above us then letting it float down, falling light and cool over us, giddy with the panicked thrill of fabric settling over our eyes, mouths, noses, giggling over Mummy's half-hearted calls for us to shut up and go to sleep. But I fell asleep first that night. And long before dawn, someone was banging on our window, yelling for Mummy to come, because Nay was missing.

∞

We went to see Nay's mother, a lumpy woman who smelled of sweat and usually shouted a lot. Our mothers were great friends. "That girl was such a help to me. What you think this country comin' to?" Her mother's voice was strangely quiet. "What I ga do? My one girl child missing."

Theresa and I exchanged a look. Nay was known for never missing anything. She didn't miss it if anyone opened a bag of chips. She didn't miss it if anyone had a new pack of Now and Later. Hand always out, always whining, "Oooh, gimmie piece?" And she had certainly not missed those cookies. Missing? We knew better.

We talked it over in bed and decided she had gone off somewhere to a big party at the beach that we had not been invited to, with red and purple balloons and chocolate cake and sandcastles and plates and plates of Sweet Mouth's cookies. We fell asleep with the taste of envy sugary in our mouths.

∞

I was sent to help Nay's mother hang out laundry first thing in the morning.

"Why her boys can't help her?" I muttered, shoving my feet into my flip-flops. Nay's four brothers ranged in age from barely walking to almost grown, and there always seemed to be at least two of them tossing pebbles at me when I passed their house.

"You don't see the woman daughter gone?" Mummy glared at me. She didn't know Nay was really on her way back home, salty and sandy and full of dessert, which we hadn't received our share of.

When I got to Nay's house, the curtains were drawn though it was past eight. I waited for what felt like an hour before Nay's oldest brother answered the door. He looked confused to see me, and held the door open. Nay's mother sat at the dining table, staring at something I couldn't see. I backed into the kitchen quietly and began loading a pile of dirty socks and shirts and underpants into the washing machine. Slowly, Nay's brothers trickled into the kitchen and past me, on their way outside. Their calls to each other began low and listless, but by the time the first spin cycle had finished, their voices were strong. Behind me, Nay's mummy stayed sitting, perfectly still.

When I was done, I came back home to wait for Theresa, who was going back to Sweet Mouth's to collect the first batch of finished jam. I pushed the door open but stood outside, where the air was moving at least. Theresa was in the front room sitting on the floor between Mummy's knees, having her hair done. She didn't look at me as Mummy raked a brush over her head.

"You wanna go down to the playground when you finish?" I asked, as she came out.

She plopped the empty box she was carrying over her head, shading herself from the sun. "Yeah."

"I'll go get the jam with you if you tell me what Sweet Mouth said."

"She ain' say nothin'." She grabbed up her box again and ran down the street, skinny legs flying. Nay's brothers celebrated her passing with a cloud of tiny stones.

∞

Every night for a week, as we lay in bed, I asked Theresa, "So you ain' ga tell me what Sweet Mouth tell you?" steadily, about every three minutes, until her breath became quiet and regular. On the seventh night, I sat up and looked at her face in the light from the open bedroom door. She lay on her belly, one arm thrown over onto my side of the bed. I saw she was half-smiling, her head turned toward the window. She was dreaming.

And then came my sleep, and then a hazy jumble—dreams of curtains puffed up with the wind, a faint tap on a window, a whisper of a word I couldn't catch over my shoulder. And then daylight and Mummy screaming *Theresa! Where Theresa? Theresa gone!*

∞

Before Mummy's screams woke me and the world shifted six clicks left, I was standing on the wharf looking at a boat, unafraid of the deep water. It was about six in the evening, the sun just low enough to be behind the boat, high enough to be right in my eyes. The top deck was crammed with people I hadn't seen in forever. Mamma Rosario, who I recognized from old photos, and Granny Davis, whose funeral was the first I ever cried at. A whole load of little girls stood at the railing in yellow dresses, laughing and waving through the bars. They were blowing me kisses. Nay was there in a crinoline skirt, and right in the centre, four heads above everyone else, was Theresa, in a great big straw hat with a brim so large it shaded her face and shoulders and some other people's too. The brim would have been knocking people in the eye if it weren't for how tall she was. I couldn't figure that out—she'd been three inches shorter than me that morning.

Theresa was waving, too, one long dark arm high above everyone else's. She wore a sapphire dress with buttons down the front and no seams at the sides, and she was calling, "See you, Brenda. See you next time, see you!" She sounded so grown. I wanted to wave back, wanted to run up the gangplank onto the boat, she'd never gone far without me before. But my feet were heavy, heavy, and my arms couldn't move. She just kept on waving with one arm, the other crooked around a huge peacock, shimmery blue, like her dress. I couldn't figure out where she stole or borrowed it from, we never had anything more exotic than a long-beaked crane in our backyard, and once, some stray Abaco parrots with red throats, their wings leafy green. And she'd never liked birds.

I wondered how she could leave me, and then the boat was sailing, though I never saw anyone pull up the gangplank—never really saw a captain, when I thought about it. None of the crew either, those big men who stand on the edges of boats and unloose them from those green wooden poles on the dock, and push off, then hop on board. I saw none of that. Just Theresa's long arm. All I knew was that she wasn't mad, but she had gone with these other people all the same, and left me alone. When I looked down I saw a white ticket for the boat, still in my hand, and while I stared at the ticket it turned into a peacock feather with a bone-white eye, and I woke up in a pant, to clattering daylight, to Mummy screaming. Beside me, the bed was rumpled and cool, the sheets empty. Not even a feather left behind.

∞

She knew it would happen, I think. She didn't tell me before-hand, just like she didn't ever tell me what it was Sweet Mouth said. In the nights after, when there was so much extra room in the bed and no one to talk to, I ran through seven or eight possibilities before settling on *Something coming what like little girls.* I could hear Sweet Mouth saying that. *Better sleep with one eye open. Better sleep in your ma bed. Something coming, something what like little girls.*

∞

I like to think her dream was a sweet one—being gathered up in soft arms, an even softer breeze kissing, kissing, kissing her forehead, kissing, kissing her nose. She must have known that Sweet Mouth was right, that there was something what loved little girls. Very much. Never before, not when she twirled around in her favourite yellow church dress that used to be mine, with the wide skirt that stood out like puffing curtains, not with her head on Mummy's lap, waiting for the baby inside Mummy's belly to kick, smelling faint lavender bath wash and scented powder and lime peel, never before had Theresa felt so loved. And so she picked up, in the dark, and she went away.

∞

On the first Monday in August, Emancipation Day, the last little girl left. Most everyone down our street was heading to the beach or some cookout or both. The people in the house in front of ours were rowing, like usual. The man was just in from working late down at the hotel and the woman had been up since before dawn. Soon there were slamming doors, and wailing pouring out like sweet-stink fruit punch from the week before. I watched from our bedroom window as their back door opened and their older girl came out.

She was a year younger than me. I saw her climb into the back seat of their car, leave the door open, legs dangling out. Scratch a bite on her knee. Inside the house, her mother hollering, "I gone call my ma an ask her if I could move back home, I can't take it any more! What you want from me?" I stepped back from the window, let the curtain fall. I lay back on the bed. The yelling stopped, after a while. Then, as quick as they started, they were laughing. I looked up at the ceiling, and reflected that adults are dumb.

The jingle of keys. The father called the girl once, twice. *She should go*, I thought, they were going for a ride, to pick up ice cream. The mother joined in; the calls became frantic. A fist on our door, a voice asking if we had seen her, but no one had come or gone from our house since that night. The girl was not in their yard, or ours, or the next. Not in a tree or under a bed. She wasn't over to the people next door, or the next or the next, or the next. And there was a wail in the air again, and in it no sweet. Only stink.

∞

The papers lied. The girls were not gone at all. Just relocated. There is no gone girls can go on one little island.

And what would one person do with all those little girls? Because it wasn't just three. They reported three, but I know there were more. Maybe twenty. Maybe fifty. Maybe a hundred more. I used to hear them in the calling hours, after the neighbours had finished their love and the air conditioning had gone to sleep. On a night without thunder or sirens, they would sing in that silence, throwing their voices up to the ceiling and down into dark corners. A chorale of little girls freer than wishing can give. Without lessons to learn or rooms to clean, dishes to wash, jars to tote, mangoes to eat. They could play all day, all night, mouths full of cookies and songs.

And they all went so neatly. I imagined them all together, all at one time. Playing Twee-lee-lee on the playground, standing in circles, hand overlaid on hand. Someone could come onto the playground easy. Someone short and dark, like them, someone with something sweet in her hands. They would scatter, at first, like pigeons, then resettle, one by one. The person could ask them if they wanted cookies. *No, we don't take cookies from strangers.* How about a song? Little girls like songs. The little girls could stare, a few nod, a few blink. One could say, *What song you know?*

Come, then she would say, *when I call, and I'll teach you. It's a song made for sweet things. Sweet things like you.*

Their little hands clap, voices tinkle and clattering, glass beads in a jar. This person has them smiling as never before. *Then,* she says, *I will take you on a trip,* her teeth glinting pretty. The little girls begin to skitter and disperse, pigeons again. They settle, this time faster.

You would like a trip, wouldn't you? She smiles and the little girls are thinking of rocking ships and soaring planes and dancing, dancing in clouds. They were lucky, then, weren't they? Not gone, but on a trip. They were not here, but they were happy, somewhere.

I dreamt of it often, the song. I could never catch the tune and always woke up to find no one there, just that strange feeling when you're sleeping alone and know someone's in the room with you, pressing their weight down on the bed.

∞

There was an arrest. An appearance in court, mothers and sisters hissing and shouting as Sweet Mouth, a small thing who could never wrestle little girls away against their will, was hustled past, sandwiched between two police officers. She was certainly not as tall as Theresa seemed in my dream. She was thinner, too. She looked like she hadn't had a good meal since before the start of the summer. I couldn't figure out why, with the rampant fruit. The cookies. All that jam. Was she so unselfish, brewing plum punch, boiling sugar and fruit for others, baking little girls cookies while her bones ate up her flesh in her dusty dark house with furniture no one ever sat in?

She could not have been cruel, since they never really found anything. Just bits of cloth in a clearing, from shirts or dresses no one recognized. And three pairs of small shoes lined up underneath her bed.

The school year after that summer was a hard one. In my class, one seat was empty. For the first month, no one sat next to me on the bus. I wanted it that way. Kept my bag beside me, saving the space for Theresa. Mothers had it hardest, I guess. Nay's mother had a child in November, a month after Mummy's stillborn. Another girl, Nay's mother told us after the baby came, and Mummy's hand had tightened around my shoulder. Nay's mother saw it and started talking about Abe Pratt's amazing comeback at church, which was very old news by then.

In our own house, Mummy began taking down Theresa's dress that used to be mine, to iron every morning. It's a shame the dress was yellowy-orange and not green or purple. Or peacock blue. When I see that dress in Mummy's curling fingers, I like to think of Theresa on the boat. How she floats and weaves and bobs above them all, waving and blowing kisses to me while I watch from the shore. I like to think of them all that way, crowded on, playing Twee-lee-lee, ducking and squeezing between our great-grandmothers.

It is a shame to think of them any other way. It would waste them.

And why waste little girls?

They can be such nice things.

LOVE

AT NIGHT, MS. BUTLER LAY IN BED and thought
over the day. After the lights were off and she had said her
Thank You Jesus Another Day Come And Gone, and made
a mental note of certain things that had to be addressed in
the morning—rising early to mark the last of the homework, stopping at the food store to pick up a bottle of punch
and a pack of cookies for after Bible Study—she was free to
recap the day's events, and eventually be guided into sleep
by the steady buzz of the neighbour's a/c and the occasional
pap of what she told herself was only firecrackers being set
off in the empty lot out back.

Today had been easy in many ways. The children had
been no more hyper than usual, and no one had celebrated
a birthday (these often resulted in a well-meaning parent

stopping by with a sheet cake topped with lardy icing and two large bottles of juice, guaranteeing a day good for nothing more than impromptu Textbook Frisbee and a flurry of visits to the headmaster's office). Tamara had come in late; that was nothing new. Nicole was getting more and more precocious; Ms. Butler had pulled her aside *again* and reminded her to go by Sandy's and buy herself a training bra, or else stay home. The children liked her assignment to group off in fours and choose a heat-free, healthy recipe they could make that Friday morning and eat as a picnic lunch together on the playing field. Angelo wasn't concentrating in class, and had to be put repeatedly in Time Out. After the fifth offence, Chris dragged the boy's desk over to the back of the room. When she asked Chris, sharply, what he was doing, he replied, "He stay in trouble, I figure he might as well jus move there." She bit back her laughter and made Chris clear a space on the board and write *I will not meddle, I will not meddle, I will not meddle.* And Melissa still wouldn't speak when called on in class.

Get paper cups and plates, she reminded herself, as she felt her eyes starting to close.

∞

Imogene—her cousin's child—was already gone when Ms. Butler woke the next morning. The girl was like a phantom. At night, she was made of invasive intangibles: the clatter of keys on the countertop when she came in late from choir practice; the bathroom door banging shut and the rush of water as she showered after basketball. In the morning, though, there was only a faint scent of synthetic citrus body spray and baby powder, empty shoes by the door an echo of her feet from days before, an abandoned bread crust on a jam-smeared plate in the sink. Ms. Butler scanned the note left under a mostly eaten bowl of grits on the counter:

Morning auntie, I hope you slept well, I have volleyball after school and coach invite us to her church youth group afterwards so I wouldn't be home til later. Love, Genie.

She crumpled up the note, dumped the bowl in the sink. Half-eaten food abandoned, half-written note full of mistakes. Didn't she know better than that? Ms. Butler sucked her teeth and gathered up a stack of exercise books, then headed for the car.

"Morning!" Ian, next door, raised his hand in greeting as she passed him. A young woman, perched on an upturned crate near him, said nothing. Ms. Butler could not make out the girl's features, but she could tell this was a new one: heavier frame, short, plump, bare feet, hot-pink nails, dark skin.

"Good morning. Your mummy doin' alright?"

"She right there." Ian stuck his head back under the hood of the car he was tinkering with. Pleasant enough young man, though she hoped Imogene would do more with her life when she got out of school. She made a mental note to speak with her about staying away from nice but aimless boys.

∞

"All right, class. What are we studying today? Who remembers?"

No hands . . . no hands . . . and then there was Shanique, predictably stiff in her chair, arm up like a flagpole, fingers wiggling for attention.

"How about someone who we haven't heard from today? Melissa?"

Melissa responded to her name with a vague shifting in her chair, eyes plastered to her open textbook. She had the page turned to the right place, "Father of Bahamian Tourism: Sir Stafford Sands." The child had probably already done tomorrow's homework too. *Shit, she could teach the class*, Ms. Butler thought, then mentally smacked her own hand for cursing. Out loud, she sighed. Shanique's movements had intensified: now, her bottom bounced slightly on her seat. She stretched her arm up so far it was a wonder it didn't pop out and drift up to the ceiling like a novelty helium balloon.

"Shanique."

"Today we are studying the forefather of tourism, Sir Stafford Sands."

"Our forefather, and the *founding father* of tourism, yes. Thank you, Shanique."

Shanique lowered her hand and folded it over the other, clasped, prim.

"Now, I'm sure you all read the textbook, so who can tell me something about Sir Stafford Sands? What was he known for?"

She let her eyes drift over the class, silent once again. They could almost use a sheet of birthday cake today. Angelo's chair was tilted back on its hind legs like a revved-up bike, his textbook nowhere in sight. Craig's head was down. *If he's asleep, he'll be drooling on his exercise book, which will be a special treat come marking time*, she thought.

"Tamara."

"Um. I don't remember."

"Who can help Tamara out? Stephanie?"

Stephanie started slightly, then pulled her textbook closer as if it had just occurred to her it might be of some use today. "Sir Stafford Sands was a founding father of an important industry in The Bahamas," she announced, her eyes glued to the page.

Nicely read, little parrot. "Yes, and what else?" she asked brightly.

A giggle from the back of the class. Angelo had managed to balance the chair on one leg, and simultaneously balance his textbook—closed—on his head. Across from him, Nicole tittered, her chest bouncing as she laughed. Ms. Butler reached for the yard ruler and brought it down on her desk with a bang. Angelo lost his balance and landed on the floor hard, his chair skidding, textbook falling open, pencils scattering. He shrank slightly as his classmates began to laugh.

"Since you finally have your book open, Angelo," she let her voice chime out over theirs like an intercom, "why don't you start reading from the top of the page."

∞

The house was empty when she got home from Bible Study. She had not wanted to take in a teenager, but at least the girl had the decency to make herself scarce, much of the time. Ms. Butler opened the fridge door and reheated a plate of the previous night's baked chicken and steamed rice, did the last of the morning's dishes. She turned on the TV, then turned it off again, opened up the textbook. "Father of Bahamian Tourism: Sir Stafford Sands." It was not her favourite chapter, not because Sir Stafford was White and had left The Bahamas soon after Blacks took over running the country, but because money bored her. The economy bored her. Tourism, unless she was the one touring, bored her. Her preferences were not important, though: the children needed to learn their history. Let them make up their own minds after.

She turned off the light and said her Thank You Jesus. In the lot behind, some boys were at it with the firecrackers again. *Pap. Pap pap. Pap pap pap.* She glanced at the clock. Almost ten. Where was Imogene, anyway? Next door, she could hear Ian arguing with someone. There was the bang of something being set down heavily, or a door closing. Probably some stupid argument with his younger brother. The mother rarely seemed to be home these days.

"What wrong with you, you think I's a ass, eh? You think I dumb?" Ian's voice was loud, hard. The mother really ought to be home, she thought. It was no way for siblings to talk to each other, and you couldn't expect children to raise themselves.

Another noise—the moving around of a chair, or a bag full of something? A high voice shouted out. Ms. Butler snapped on the light and reached for the textbook. Might as well get to planning next week's classes, as there was no sleep to be had yet that night.

∞

She woke with a start. Her glasses askew, her headscarf had come off, the bedside light was still on. Ms. Butler sat up and settled her glasses on her face. Squinted at the clock: five after eleven.

Thunk. Thunk. Thunk. She repositioned her scarf, ran a hand over her face. Familiar sound, but she couldn't place it. What was that?

Thunk. Thunk. Thunk.

Imogene. Had she come in last night? Ms. Butler opened her bedroom door and poked her head out. The hallway light had been turned off, the girl's door closed. She looked up toward the front of the house. The chain was on the door. The girl's worn sneakers stood at the end of a row of abandoned shoes, the heel of one wedged up against the side of the other. "Hmph."

She walked down the hall and nudged the shoes out of the pathway to the front door, then returned to her room. She turned her sheets back properly and lay down. She began to say her Thank You Jesus, then remembered she had done it already, and turned out the light.

Thunk. Thunk. Thunk.

There, again. She parted the curtains and peered out. She could not make out his face in the dark, but knew it must be the neighbour's younger boy, basketball in hand. He was bouncing the ball, then aiming it against the wall, where it ricocheted back to him. *Thunk.*

"Ryan! You ain' see what time it is?"

He bounced the ball again. He had not heard her.

She could hear a TV on in the house next door, then, "Ian, stop, man, leave me!" A high, shrill voice that made her think, strangely, of Nicole and those new, untethered breasts, pointing and shuddering under her thin yellow school blouse. Another low, heavy sound from inside the house next door. The ball again. *Thunk.* "Leave me, Ian! Stop it!"

Nicole indeed. Ms. Butler shook her head and brushed a scattering of goosebumps off her arms. She let the curtain fall.

∞

Ms. Butler woke to a crick in her back. Fumbled the alarm silent, sat up. In making the bed, she discovered the *Story of The Bahamas* textbook tangled in the sheets. No wonder she had slept funny. It was open, and the front cover was bent down the middle. She bent it the other way to try to fix it, shaking her head at her carelessness.

∞

At lunch, she opened her mark book. Yes, she would need to call in one or two parents next week. Sarah was failing English, Science, and Math. Tamara had almost enough Lates to be granted a green slip. She glanced out the window, toward the playground. Between the slatted shutters, she recognized a few of her pupils. There was Angelo, ringleader of a game of pocking. She watched him snatch a tennis ball out of mid-air like a dog, then swing his arm back and let fly. "*Itch!*" The ball bounced off another boy's leg. The victim yelped, rubbed the spot. Angelo caught the ball up again, relishing his perfect aim.

"Y'all boys ain' suppose to be playin' that!" she called through the shutters. Angelo's head turned—had he heard her? His arm swung back again.

A smattering of girls ran by the windows, then, a few moments later, into the classroom. Patrice, Monique, Nicole. The latter was predictably unbound beneath her blouse. The girls' faces glistened with light sweat. They fanned themselves as they fell into their seats.

Ms. Butler cleared her throat. "Excuse me. Recess isn't over."

"But it's hot. Can we come in early?" Monique piped up.

"Find a shady tree. You only have ten more minutes."

The girls sighed, shuffling back out again, drained of all the hustle that had propelled them in moments before. Ms. Butler watched them settle on a patch of grass opposite the door. They had begun to give off that aroma, dirty sweet musk. The talk on hygiene was usually reserved for the grade sevens. She made a mental note to ask the guidance counsellor in for an early presentation. Nicole swatted the air, fending off some pest she couldn't see. There it was again, that unfettered shaking. The child might as well have stowed Jell-O under her clothes. Ms. Butler walked toward the open door. Some things couldn't wait.

"Nicole."

The girl turned her head. "Yes, Ms. Butler?"

"Come up here, please."

The girl separated herself from her friends. She was quite pretty, in a stubborn, rowdy way. Her hair was slicked back, accentuating her high forehead, velvety-smooth skin.

"Yes?"

Mrs. Butler cleared her throat.

"Yes, ma'am?"

"Nicole, what did I tell you about the right way to come dressed for school?"

Nicole stared back at her, narrow eyes as wide as they could get.

"You don't remember?"

"No, ma'am."

"You're old enough to be wearing a bra. Matter of fact, you're too old *not* to wear a bra." She glanced down at the girl's chest, intruding into the conversation, mangoes ripening in December, abrupt and out of season. "You're a young lady now, you can't go out with your breasts shaking about like that."

The girl folded her arms over her chest. *Like that would hide it*, Ms. Butler thought.

"Do I need to send another note home to your mummy asking her to help you dress properly, or are you old enough to handle it yourself?"

"Yes."

"Yes, what?"

"Yes, I could handle it."

She frowned. "Go on, then."

The girl flounced back to her bundle of friends. They clustered around her, whispering and glancing back, and bustled away from the classroom. *How long*, Ms. Butler thought, *before I have the privilege of teaching that girl's first baby?*

∞

It was dark once again when Ms. Butler returned home. She began unloading the paper plates and cups from the back seat, then thought better of it. She would only have to pack them into the car again in the morning. She would need to bring mixing bowls as well, and some extra sheets for the picnic lunch. She shut the car door, listening as it echoed lightly through the street.

In the next yard, the radio played. She glanced over. "Evening!"

Ian's head appeared from beneath the car's raised hood. He lifted his hand in greeting. "Night, Ms. Butler." He returned to the hood of his car. The plump girl was back again, this time leaning against the front of the house. Ms. Butler remembered something she was to have mentioned to him. The noise in the night.

"Hey, Ian." She walked over to the fence.

He emerged from the hood once again. "Yes, ma'am."

"Your mummy outta town?"

"Yes, ma'am, she gone to Miami for a month."

"You think you could keep the volume down after hours?"

He shifted, uncomfortable. "Oh, right." He ran a hand over the back of his head.

"Your brother was playing ball after eleven last night, I could hardly sleep."

"Right, right." His face relaxed into a sort of smile. "Of course, Ms. Butler, I ga tell him keep it down. Sorry bout that."

"Alright." She glanced over toward the house. "So this your girlfriend, eh?"

"Yes, ma'am, this Antonia."

The girl said nothing. *No manners, girl*, she thought. "Look like she here a lot."

"Yeah, her grammy in Long Island so she stayin' here so she don't have to be alone. Ain' safe, ya see?"

"I see." She cast another look over the girl, overflowing her tank top, shorts cut high on her fleshy legs. Amazing how some girls were raised with no respect. Anyway, it wasn't her business. "Well, you have a good night."

∞

Again, she woke, sudden and sharp. She listened for the basketball; nothing. Then *crash!* She sat up. It had come from next door.

A man's voice, raised. "What he name? Hey? Hey?"

"He ain' name nothing." The same shrill voice, Nicole again. "Ain' no he, man, I ain' lyin'!"

Another crash, and a thick, meaty sound. Then a shriek.

"Shut fuckin' up, ya lyin' bitch. Get." He spat the word, as though he were chasing a stray dog out of the yard. "Get. Get out this house."

"Ian, what wrong with you?" No, it wasn't Nicole. It was the girlfriend. What was her name? Then another of the thick sounds, dull, insulated. "Stop! What wrong with you?"

Ms. Butler froze. Where were the girl's parents? And then, suddenly, now, in all of this, *thunk, thunk, thunk.* She parted the curtains, peered out. The house next door was closed up, drapes pulled tight, but there, in the middle of the awful din, the fool younger brother, his form shadowy in the dark, practicing at—well, it had to be after midnight now. She thought to call the police. *Thunk. Thunk. Thunk.*

The boy made a three-quarter swivel now, basketball in hand, facing his back door. *Thunk. Thunk. Thunk.* Basketball on concrete patio. Then, the ball was up to his chest, and, quick, he thrust it toward his house. It hit the door with a heavy, hollow thump, then bounded, obedient, back into his hands. He shoved it out again, harder now.

"Who's that? Who the fuck that is at my door? Who you call?" Ian barked. The back door opened just as the ball returned to the younger boy's hands. Ms. Butler ducked down so she wouldn't be seen, but kept watching. Ian's frame backlit, shadows on his face. The two figures seemed to be staring one another down.

The door slammed shut. The boy in the yard, ball clasped in his hands, charged. He sent the ball hurtling toward the door, a single *thunk* shaking it in its frame. The ball bounced, then again, lower, and rolled, coming to rest on the grass.

The house next door fell quiet. The boy stood in the shadows, only the tips of his shoes visible in the yellow glare from the outside light. He turned for the gate. Where could he be going this time of night? Shouldn't be anywhere but in his own house, though she could understand why he wouldn't want to be there. The light caught his face, then. Long, oval, smooth.

Imogene.

Ms. Butler watched her slip out of the neighbours' yard and into their own. She let the curtain fall. She heard the unlocking of her own back door—had she given the girl the back door key?—and a trail of steps, fading almost to silence, then, almost inaudibly, the opening and closing of the girl's bedroom door. In the lot behind, a single firecracker. *Pap.*

∞

Ms. Butler observed the children on the lawn as they ate their picnic lunch of chicken salad, green salad, ginger beets, sandwiches. She felt her eyelids threatening to close, then gave herself a little shake.

"Angelo!" She waved to the boy, who had strayed to the far end of the field where the school ended and the empty lot began. Why couldn't he just stay where he was supposed to be? "Angelo!" He glanced back, then turned away. "Someone go get him."

The girl jumped up, her still unharnessed body moving to its own rhythm. "Not you, Nicole. You finish your plate." The girl sank back down.

Angelo continued along the edge of the fence. He had found a stick. It made a clinking sound as he ran it across the metal, raising a monotone song.

She would need to call Nicole's mother in after all.

∞

She sat at the dining table, going over the Social Studies homework. *Sir Stafford Sands was an important man. He was famously for making tourism a popular job.* Sighed. The next essay began as creatively. *Sir Stafford Sands was both an influential and a controversial figure in Bahamian history.* Straight from the textbook.

The back door opened, afternoon spilling in.

"Hi, Auntie!" Imogene dropped her schoolbag on the table.

"Mmm." Irritation flickered. Doubtless it had been on the floor, the grass, some sticky chair at school, through the course of the day. Didn't the child know better?

"You goin' to prayer meeting?"

The cheerful inquiry vexed her. Who was Imogene to ask Ms. Butler, a grown woman, about where she planned to be? "You was out pretty late last night."

"Yeah, youth group ran little late. We had a good discussion going."

"You only went to youth group?"

Imogene gazed back at her, eyes wide and clear. "Yes, Auntie Sam."

Why had she agreed to take the girl in at all? Lying, bad manners—Deb should have stepped in, she was just as much family, had already raised a son. Ms. Butler glanced out the door, which the child had left open. "And where you goin' now?" She caught a glimpse of Ian's girlfriend, lingering by the fence. Imogene reached for her tennis shoes. "Just next door to play ball."

Later, she would not recall how she had leaped across the room so fast. She would not be able to say how the textbook had wound itself up like a baton, so tight, or why exactly she had been so angry. Only that Imogene's hand had reached out before Ms. Butler even made contact, swatted the book out of her grip, sent it bouncing off the wall. The girl had held her gaze then, assassin-steady, even as Ms. Butler shook with rage. The girl's eyes were calm. Nothing bound her.

Imogene was first to look away. She left without a word, a second glance, the back door clicking shut behind her.

Her, the child Ms. Butler had brought up from small. She looked at her empty hand, then down at the book on the floor. The girl did not respect her. Almost worse, she did not feel anything else for her either. Certainly not love.

There was a sound outside. Ms. Butler turned to the window. Imogene had not gone far. She and Ian's girlfriend were, indeed, playing ball on the wide slab of concrete next door. The girlfriend was quick with the ball, agile despite her thick frame. Imogene grabbed it back, bent her knees to make a shot. So steady, so easy. As though nothing had ever been wrong.

Ms. Butler wanted to lie down. She could close her eyes, let sleep come, give in to it through her marking hour, sleep straight through the prayer meeting. Outside, one of the girls shouted. She opened the door, stepped outside. They were almost good. Imogene turned, shielding the ball from her opponent; the girlfriend stole it back, then took aim, and jumped. Her large breasts lifted and fell as she moved, free.

At the front of the yard, Ian's car struggled to start. She heard it shut off, then a clank as the hood opened.

The girls slapped hands, laughing. Ms. Butler brought her hand up to her own chest, her breath tight and slow.

"Hey, Ms. Butler."

She turned toward his voice. There he was, between the shrubs, arm raised in greeting. The girls sounded further away now. Ms. Butler hesitated, then waved back.

AUNTIES

MISS PETTY TUTORED EVERY Wednesday afternoon. She began each session with a prayer, which Edmond routinely interrupted because he liked to take a longer route to her house from school. When Miss Petty heaved herself to her feet to let him in, her voice would shift and she often missed a word or two of the Lord's Prayer. If these words happened to be *give us this day/our daily bread*, Marcia would think of Miss Petty's large, soft body and snicker, and Miss Petty would say, *No, no, no, no, no. This is a solemn time. Y'all start over again.* She would wave Edmond over to his seat while continuing to lead our chorused bid for forgiveness. This was followed by a half hour each of Math, English, Science, and Social Studies. Miss Petty believed in hands-on learning, and in feeding people well. We reviewed the solar system with the aid of lemon shortbreads and melty almond macaroons of varying sizes. I grew to relish fractions, since she illustrated them by dividing a slab of double-layer chocolate cake into halves, then quarters, then eighths.

My parents both worked late, so I stayed on with Miss Petty after the other children had left. In that hour, Miss Petty baked, and this was when the real learning began. I followed her into the sun-lit kitchen, where the counter-tops were crowded with quietly expanding heaps of dough. Sometimes a cupboard door had been left open, revealing jars of jewelled raisins and dried cranberries, and chocolate chips whose aroma seemed to permeate through the glass. The plastic bin by the fridge was always stacked high with green-gold coconuts. Six months into our tutoring sessions, I worked up the courage to ask Miss Petty how she got the flakes out of the coconuts. She looked over at me, her face lit up with surprise, but she only said, "I'll show you next time." The following week, Miss Petty took me out onto the back doorstep. She was armed with her machete; I held the hammer while she stripped the nut of its green out-side, then drained its water into a tall Tupperware cup. The hammer was then used to split the husk open. Two of the nuts yielded a clean break, but the third stuck to the thick brown shell. In the kitchen, we worked in silence for several minutes, coaxing the white flesh away from the shell with a pair of butter knives.

"When we need coconut, Mummy buys a bag of flakes from Super Value down the road," I confessed finally. "She hides it in the back of the freezer so Daddy doesn't find it."

Miss Petty chuckled, but not unkindly—I could tell she didn't think my mother was a lesser kind of woman for baking with something that came in a package labelled *desiccated*. Her laugh made me feel as though she understood my mother's secrecy, and, more importantly, that she felt I did too. "It's a lot of work, and your mummy's so busy." She dried her hands on her skirt. "Well, that coconut water can't drink itself." Miss Petty divided the water between two glasses. She took out a big bottle of some brown liquid and splashed a little in one of the cups.

"Can I try some too?"

She considered my request, then leaned the bottle over and dribbled a few drops into my portion. I drank. Beneath the sweetness of the water was a burning, lurking roughness that made me screw up my face. I understood that this was another mature secret, and finished the glass while her stand mixer whirred. I giggled a lot for the next half hour, and she gave me two garlicky corn fritters and a mint before sending me home.

The week before report cards came out, Miss Petty's lesson ran late. Marcia's eyes slid over to the clock above the bookshelf. Five thirty-five. A minute later, a car eased into the driveway, its headlights illuminating the dining room. Miss Petty didn't blink. At five forty, Clarissa began sliding her pencil and ruler back into her case. Miss Petty seemed not to notice. Edmond sighed weightily.

"I think my mummy's outside," Mark said finally, at five forty-two.

"Go ahead, baby," Miss Petty said, not moving from the table. Mark grabbed his bag and bolted.

Clarissa seized the opportunity. "I have to go too," she said, closing up her book. "My daddy said not to be late."

"Oh, we did go over a little. See y'all next week." Miss Petty slid her glasses off and set them down on the table. "And don't forget to let me see those report cards next week."

The others were gone quickly. As I put my books away, I thought of my own empty, silent house. Last night my mother had picked up takeout from the Chinese takeaway beside the food store. Tonight would be leftovers, or else salads and reheated chicken from the deli. My stomach emitted a long, discouraged whine. Today, we had reviewed types of triangles and women gaining the right to vote. Neither principle had involved an edible component. I took my time zipping up my schoolbag. I felt funny, today, hanging around, the charge of my classmates' clatter and scurry still in the air.

"Well. I sure could use another set of tastebuds with these ricotta pastries, Lydia. I already kept you all late today, but maybe you can taste one and tell me what you think they need." Miss Petty looked back at me from the kitchen doorway, a spoon already in her hand. I pushed my chair back, and as I followed her, I felt I had never loved anyone more.

∞

"Sandwiches?" My father scrutinized the plate in front of him as though it had sprouted a pair of eyes.

My mother slid into her seat. "They had extras from an event at work. Saved me having to make a stop on the way home."

Daddy pushed the dish away. "I don't want someone else's leftovers."

I felt my mother bristle. I picked up the triangle closest to me. I recognized the filling: processed cheese, with a layer of mayonnaise and a slice of onion. I took a bite and thought of the phyllo parcel Miss Petty had slid onto a plate for me earlier that day. The pastry layers had been delicate and crisp, the inside creamy and hot.

"What did you learn in your tutoring class today?" Mummy nibbled at what looked to be bologna with a slice of pale tomato.

"Um . . . triangles." The pastry had crunched, giving way against my teeth. How could something so thin and crisp hold a filling? It was a mystery.

"My mother used to have a hot meal on the table every night." Daddy pushed his chair back and strode into the kitchen. We could hear him then rummaging around in the cupboards, as if they might magically supply something steamy and flavourful. "*And* she worked," he added, pointedly.

"Maybe you should have married her." Mummy's murmur was less hushed than it should have been.

"What do you mean triangles?" My father's voice reverberated from the kitchen. "You learned your shapes in grade one."

"Um—well, we do fractions too." There had been some sort of cheese inside the pastry. Ricotta, and something that started with a *p*. I swallowed a glob of my sandwich and took a gulp of water. "Last week Miss Petty showed us how you can use fractions to cut a cake."

Daddy returned with an orange. "I'm paying for your grades to come up so you can eat cake?"

"Don't pick on her, Theo."

"I better see some As on your report card." Daddy jammed a thumbnail into the orange's skin. "Or it may be time to cut the tutoring altogether."

"Stop picking at the girl." Mummy inspected her sandwich, then extracted a piece of lettuce leaf from its folds.

I could hear Miss Petty clucking over the limp romaine. "A step above iceberg," she had said, a few weeks back. "There's no reason to eat boring vegetables. You see this?" She'd held up a bundle of frilly greens. "Wild arugula. The colour means it's got more nutrients, and it has a nice bite. Here, try it." I hesitated, but nothing Miss Petty offered had ever disappointed me. I tore off a piece and put it into my mouth. It started off peppery, but the heat never took off.

"I'm sure she's learning something there." Mummy's voice brought me back. "Aren't you?"

I nodded. I wanted to tell my parents that Miss Petty taught me plenty. How white sugar would brown when heated, turn from grit into liquid, let itself be drizzled, then harden again. That you could put raw almonds into a blender and they would turn first to flour, then yield into a paste like peanut butter, only sweet. How, when a two-pound bag gave out at the bottom and sent chocolate chips chattering onto the floor, instead of cursing your bad luck, you could scoop them up, laughing, dunk them in a bowl of cold water, and make a triple batch of cookies, filling the air with cocoa and laughter.

My father drained his water and set the glass down hard. "Well?"

"We're practicing adverbs," I said. "Like, a double-glazed cake. Or a creamy lemon tart."

Daddy shot my mother a scathing look. "You're right. That's worth my money."

Mummy reached for another sandwich, then set it on my plate. When she spoke, her voice was a sad whisper. "Those are adjectives," she said.

∞

There was much fuss as Miss Petty had us all bring out our little brown envelopes, which were meant to arrive home properly sealed, though Marcia had obviously broken hers open. Not that it mattered. She had only Bs and As; her parents would not care that she had disobeyed the rule. I kept my envelope in my hands under the dining table.

"Let's see how you did!" Miss Petty reached out toward me. She was wearing a ring. I had never seen her wear jewellery. I looked at her plump, smooth hand. I held mine back.

"She don't wanna open it," Marcia chimed up. "Her daddy ga get mad if he don't see it first. She knows all she has is Cs and Ds, and her daddy ga pull her out of tutoring."

I kicked her under the table.

"Bring it to show me next week," Miss Petty said, opening up the Math textbook. "And we'll finish ten minutes early today, to make up for going late last week." She leaned over to me. "Lydia, I have to head out this evening, so I have to ask you—"

Heat flooded my face as I picked up my pencil. "Yes, ma'am," I hurried over her words. "I know."

After class, I followed the others outside. The afternoon felt bare, raw.

"Miss Petty gat date tonight." Edmond shifted his bag onto his shoulder.

"She so fat," Marcia said. "Who you think would like her?" None of us responded, because Miss Petty being fat was not news, and besides, all of us knew plenty of fat married ladies, like our principal, whose car rose four or five inches when she got out of it each morning, and

Pastoress Major, who had at least seven children, and delivered her sermons at the Holy Gospel Chapel seated across the better part of a small pew on the stage.

I peered down the road to see if my parents' cars were outside our house yet. Daddy's was, luckily, even though it was early still. I broke away from the other two and hurried home. I wondered how I had missed my father going by. As I walked up the driveway, I noticed that the curtains were drawn, although it was still light outside. I banged on the door but no one answered, so I used my key, fumbling with it at first. He would remember the report card. He would open it, he would not like what he saw.

Inside, the house had the strange smell of a visitor: different soap, foreign perfume. I took off my shoes and walked down to the bedrooms, the report card crumpled in my hand. Perhaps if I showed only one of my parents at a time, it would be better. Daddy could be mad first, and Mummy after, and thus, their wrath would be dispersed. Just outside my parents' room, I caught a whiff of something familiar, sweet. Vanilla, and melted chocolate. Miss Petty? My breath caught. I opened the door, just a crack. She couldn't be here.

Two hushed voices. Mummy was home after all. My parents sounded happy, like people on TV. Daddy laughed. His voice seemed strange, different. When had he last laughed? Then I panicked. They were happy—without me.

"You hear something?" A quick rustling, then my father appeared at the door.

"Lydia! What you doin' home already?" He looked at his wrist. He was not wearing his watch.

"What happened to Mummy's car?"

"Go in your room. Go do your homework, okay?"

"I did it. I just come from Miss Petty."

"Well, go watch TV then."

"It's before seven." I held out my report card to him.

"Ian?" A woman's voice. "Everything okay?"

It was not my mother. Daddy turned back into the room. He opened his mouth; his face looked the way it did just before he swore. "Ain' nothing," he called instead. The woman came into view. She was short and plump, and wore jeans and a low red top. I wondered what her job was. Neither Mummy nor any of our teachers ever wore jeans on a weekday. The woman started when she saw me.

"Oh, glory!"

"Lydia, this your Auntie Joan." Daddy's voice shook inexplicably. "She just givin' us a surprise visit."

The woman darted back out of sight. It was the first time anyone had ever appeared frightened of me.

"It's a surprise, okay? So don't tell Mummy. Okay? You could keep a secret? For me?"

My father waited for me to nod. I nodded.

"Good girl. Gone, go watch TV, Auntie Joan just havin' a nap, she ain' feelin' too good. Gone, go turn on some cartoons."

I moved away from the door, which then closed gently. I didn't know where to go. I wanted to go back to Miss Petty's, to the smell of sugar, to the bowls full of smooth dough and the bins of coconut, the fridge flowing over with guavas and mangoes and pineapples sent over from her sister on the island, the quiet of her home after classes were over, the way the air was always hot from the oven, yet clear from something I couldn't quite name. I pushed myself toward the front of the house, not sure how my legs got me there, out the door, no key in hand, down the concrete pavement, past house tree truck house garbage house house. I was almost at the end of the road when a car horn slowed me. Miss Petty, sandwiched into her old Volkswagen.

"Where you goin'? I thought your daddy was home."

I shook my head.

"That ain' his car in the driveway?" She was wearing her hair down from its usual tiny ponytail. She had curled it around her face.

I nodded.

"What happen, Lydia, your tongue broke?" She had on lipstick, a dainty pink.

"Yes, ma'am."

"Lydia. Where you goin'?"

I couldn't say. She shook her head.

"Well, how I suppose to enjoy my evening out with you roamin' up and down the street? Come on, get in."

She unlocked her passenger door. I slid inside and slammed the door shut. The car light stayed on, persistent bright.

"It's your—" She stopped short.

I followed her gaze to the brown envelope, jammed in the closed door. I grabbed the envelope and pulled. There was a rip—quick, bitter. I stared at the envelope in my hand, the report card exposed through the large tear. There was some way this was all my fault, but I couldn't be sure how.

Miss Petty lifted the envelope off my lap so light it could have been a butterfly rising. "Let's see," she said, and slipped the card out. "One, no, two Bs . . ."

She drove us down, very slowly, toward my house. Daddy was in the street, his shirt unbuttoned, no tie. Miss Petty stopped. I could feel her looking past me, at him. She rolled down my window. She could have said some reassuring, adult thing, "She's right here, Mr. Saunders," or made a sort of joke, "You missing something?" There was silence.

"Miss P. You dress right up," my father said. I couldn't bring myself to look at him.

Miss Petty reached past me and held the report card out to him. As he took it, she made a sound in her throat, the one she usually reserved for Edmond. She squeezed my hand. Her fingers were soft. "Good night, Lydia." Usually, when she said goodbye at the end of a tutoring class, her voice lifted like she was singing a little song. Tonight, her tone was low. I wished I could hunker into her passenger seat, sit with her in the restaurant, lean my head against her shoulder during a movie, just ride around until I fell asleep. Even if she sounded that serious, that sad, all night.

"Come, Lydia." Daddy stepped back from the car, waiting. As I opened the door, the envelope fluttered down to the road. My father stooped to pick it up. We stood and watched, together, as Miss Petty drove away. Her car's brake lights winked as she slowed at the end of the corner, and then she disappeared. When we stepped inside the house, the woman was gone. Soon after, Mummy came home. I snuck a glance at my report card, which someone had placed on the table. My teacher's slanted black pen-strokes began to thicken and blur. I looked away. My parents passed it between themselves, faces longer than a Baptist funeral. After our meal of sweet and sour meats and fried rice, my mother sent me to bed. I lay in the dark, waiting for someone to scold me, but no one came. I listened for raised voices. There was darkness, and on the other side of the wall, in my parents' bedroom, all was quiet.

∞

Sometime after that, my mother began to make plans for me and her to move out. I asked her where I would go to for tutoring, and she said something about it not making too much difference, there wouldn't be money for that, and

Miss Petty was going back to school to be a chef anyway. That afternoon, I asked Miss Petty if this was true. She was quiet for what felt like a long time. Behind us, a pot of water simmered, sending cinnamon and mace into the air. Miss Petty peeled an apple. Its skin unfolded like a flattened snake. I held my breath.

"Things change," she said, as she gutted the apple of its core. "But I'll always have time for my boys and girls." Her phone rang, then. She set the ribbon of green down on the counter. "Can you throw that away?" She answered the call. Her voice lifted like sunlight rising.

I stood in the kitchen alone. I knew what she said was not true. My mother and I would live somewhere different, and someone else would share Miss Petty's afternoon glass of bittersweet. Daddy would shut himself in the bedroom with Auntie Joan every day and laugh and laugh. Nothing would be the same. I flung the peel into the pot first, then the core, and watched the black seeds rise. Why would Miss Petty lie? I had thought better of her.

THE WATER

"DIDN'T SEE THIS ONE COMING. Big storm deep in winter." The woman squeezed between us and the soup shelf, then frowned at the bare shelves. "They almost out of Chicken Noodle already?"

"'The prudent sees danger and hides.'" Mummy reached past the woman for the last two cans. "Excuse me."

"Miss, you don't see me here?" The woman eyed our shopping basket, then turned back to the display. Up on the top shelf, I could see a few less favourable flavours, Cream of Spinach, Green Bean. "You need all that? Look like you have ten cans!"

"'But the simple,'" my mother continued, "'go on and suffer.'" She turned to me. "Get some peas too."

At the front, we waited to pay amidst the push of early shoppers. Some, like us, were in Sunday best: patent leather shoes, net-trimmed hats, stockings, lined dresses, lace-edged socks. Others seemed to have rolled out of bed and into Big Value. A girl with uncombed hair bumped into me as she reached for three candy bars. My mother set her narrow shoulders firmly, feet slightly further apart than usual, ready to withstand a jostling. Outside was breezy and bright. We were not quite in the storm's path, but it had veered east overnight. After last year, no one wanted to take a chance.

∞

"The Lorddd-hha! Has-a never looked *kindly* on the *ways* of the INFIDEL!"

"Amen!" A few regulars added fuel to the flame.

Beside me, in the back row, Michael leaned over to Jeanne and whispered. She giggled, then covered her mouth, muffling the sound. Almost as if in response, the pastor increased his volume.

"Now I know some of us *know* people, I'm not gonna say we do it ourselves, I'm not gonna give-a voice-a to such-a wickedness, but we all *know* people, don't we?" He shifted from foot to foot. "Liars!"

"Speak, preacher."

"Cheaters!"

"Yes!"

"Adulterers and gossips."

"Mmmmhmmm."

He wiped his forehead with a tissue. "Some of us even know people who-a *dabble* in the Darkness, who-a *deal* in the Voodoo, as they call it in *some* places!"

The church murmured. He was working up to something. On Michael's left side, I sat completely still, aware that, even from her post in the front row, Mummy had ways of keeping tabs on us.

"You know what God-a calls it? ALL of it?"

Michael leaned over and began scribbling something on the paper Jeanne had balanced on her hymnal.

"He calls-a it . . ." and here, Pastor left a small silence. The congregation was silent too, gathering breath to leap into choreographed *amen*-ing and *that's right*-ing. Michael lifted his pen. *Fun*, he'd written.

My laugh was a short bark. Jeanne, though, must have had a mint in her mouth; there was plenty of spit, which stretched her laugh into a single syllable that extended across ten or twelve seconds. She realized both her volume and her unfortunate timing too late; the sound could not be halted. It had to run its course. It did; the noise elongated, then sprang back on itself, bouncing off the walls and dark rafters above. Mr. Adams' dust-grey head, which had been bobbing in gentle repose in the pew in front of ours, snapped up. A new, fuller silence followed. This was broken when an usher, standing in the aisle nearby, leaned across three people and smacked Jeanne firmly in the back of her head. At the front of the church, Mummy's powder-blue hat sat firm and stalwart. She did not turn around.

"I can-a SEE," the pastor began again, "that some amongst us dis*agree!*"

"No, no, no!"

"Keep going, Pastor!"

The crowd was awake with indignation.

"But I TELL you, these ailments are a problem that *is* amongst us, even within our midst. Within, perhaps, OUR OWN HEARTS!"

"That's right, brother," the woman at the end of our row, young, not much older than Michael, shouted. She then shot a withering look down the pew; it was directed toward Jeanne, I thought, but it seemed to land only as far as me. I looked away.

"And not only those more common transgressions of dishonesty, of the brief moral stray." He glanced behind himself, a vision of the backslider. "You can't *tell* me that with all these—all these *changes* we have," he lowered his voice, looking into the congregation, "that there is no *moral* change at play!"

"Speak it, brother."

"That's right!"

"And I can-a tell you, when the Israelites got mixed up with those other nations, with the Canaanites and the

Perizzites and the Amalekites and the this-ites and the that-ites, they got TURNED AWAY from their God—"

Beside me, Jeanne rubbed the back of her head. The swat must have still been stinging her.

"—and they got led away from the goodness of the glory of their God, into the worshipping of idols, into the sleeping with the enemy, even sparing the lives of those God told them to slaughter. Church, they allowed *others* to lead them away from the WORD of GOD!"

Jeanne stood up, squeezed past Michael and then me. Her navy-blue Mary Janes had thick heels that clacked on hard floors; the red plush carpet down the aisles ate up the noise. The door to the sanctuary creaked open, then clicked shut after her.

"Mummy, he ain' finish talk yet," a little girl said in her best Talk Quiet In Service whisper.

"I'm running people outta the church today. You see that? You see that, flock?"

The flock saw.

"But I'm just getting warmed up!" he rasped, stepping out from behind the podium. "See, we need these words more than EVER today. You see, the book says there shall be signs and wonders." His voice became inviting, as though he wanted us to lean forward, listen close. "Mark my words, brethren. It is no *coincidence* that we are seeing strange things even in nature. Hurricane season has always been in the summer. By man's calendar, we say June to

November. This storm has no business rising up in the middle of January. Sometimes things come to get our attention. Congregation, don't you sleep."

It was getting hot. I shifted, eyeing the sealed windows. The air conditioner hummed but it wasn't doing much good. We were only forty-five minutes into the 10 a.m. service, but it felt like the afternoon was kicking in. I could feel the room expanding, contracting. In front of us, Mrs. Munroe's foot tapped against the floor. I reached for Michael's bulletin, which dangled from his fingers, and used it to try to move the air around my face. The Spider-Man he had begun to doodle around one edge wiggled before my eyes. I leaned back into the pew. At the end of the row, the young woman shifted in disapproval. Up front, the pastor continued to speak. People murmured their agreement. I looked up at the fan, splicing air, slicing words. I closed my eyes.

∞

"Never been so ashamed of y'all as I was today," Mummy said over dinner. "Michael, tell us what you learned today. If you even heard anything with all your shenanigans."

Michael muttered something to the bones on his plate.

"How about you, Jeanne? Nothing?"

Across from me, Jeanne kept her eyes on the thin slip of tablecloth between her plate and her dress.

"He shouldn't talk fool if he want people to stay in his church," Jeanne said. Deep in the kitchen, there was a clatter of dishes. I froze a moment—I had forgotten Ms. Louise was still here. Jeanne's words must have shocked her, too.

"Louise?" Mummy's voice was like an extended elastic band about to split from the strain. Perhaps she had forgotten too.

Jeanne's mother appeared, flour on the front of her skirt. Her gloved hands glistened with water and soap bubbles. "Mrs. Deveaux?"

"Take the afternoon off." Mummy seemed to look through Jeanne's mother, as though she was addressing a slab of glass that had been granted the power of comprehension. "Y'all can go."

The woman blinked. She slipped off the rubber gloves, then reached for the pink cotton scarf tied around her head, as though she had forgotten it was there and did not wish to be caught looking so.

"I'll give you all a ride home. Jeanne, wrap up some food for Ms.—for you and your mummy to take," my father said quietly.

"That's alright, Mr. Deveaux." Ms. Louise's voice was soft. "We can walk."

After she had left through the kitchen door, Jeanne trailing behind her, Mummy turned back to me. "What you learned today? Besides how *not* to act?"

"Enough, Brenda," Daddy said.

"Hmph," Mummy said, putting down her spoon.

∞

Later that night, I tiptoed out into the living room. I could hear my parents snoring, each in their own pitch and tone. I couldn't sleep.

The television lit Michael's face up in starts and stops. A young girl was cowering in terror while someone much larger loomed in the foreground, only their shadow visible. He stared unblinkingly at the television, as though he didn't realize I was there.

I sat down on the armrest. "What this is?"

Michael stirred. "Some movie."

There was an ad on now. Exuberant women celebrating the effectiveness of air-sanitizing spray. He switched to the weather channel. The reporter gestured at an animated map that showed a series of storm shadows cast in reverse, hurtling toward the larger land mass below us.

"Hurricane Raquel," the weatherman said, "is now moving *away* from The Bahamas. It has gained strength, and is now expected to make landfall as a dangerous Category 5 on Tuesday in—"

"To God be the glory." Mummy's voice made us both turn. The TV's haze tinged her skin blue. "It'll miss us, then."

"Predictions are now expecting it to cause mass devastation—"

Michael snapped the TV off and tossed the remote onto the sofa. It landed soundlessly.

"Pray it doesn't hurt anybody." Mummy's words trailed back to us as she turned for her room again.

I stood up. Was she giving us an order, or speaking to herself? For a moment, I felt the carpet shift beneath me. No, I had imagined it. I moved myself forward, one foot, one foot, to go back to bed.

∞

I woke Monday morning to find my room buzzing. Mummy moved about like a dervish, gathering up too-small dresses and discoloured sheets.

"Church having a donations drive," she announced, from deep in my closet.

"What for?" I rubbed my eyes.

"Once this storm hit, those people down south ga need everything. Time for us to let our light shine."

I picked out a handful of shirts that no longer fit and laid them at the edge of my unmade bed. The armpits were stained a permanent yellow, but people who were waiting for the storm to flatten their homes and flood their land might not care about sweat marks. I peeked into the hallway.

Michael's door was open, several pairs of shoes piled beside a stack of clothes. Apparently Mummy had taken her whirlwind in there too. Then someone screamed.

Michael burst out of his room. We both froze a moment, before we shot into our parents' room. No one was there; the bed was made, the bathroom door closed. My heart was pounding. I banged on the door. I could hear Mummy inside; she was making a low, moaning noise.

"Mummy, you hurt yourself?" I rattled the knob. It wouldn't turn.

"Mummy, what happened? Open the door!" Michael called from behind me.

I could hear the tub filling, water splashing into water.

"It's alright," she said, in a voice that was not.

The door clicked open. Mummy was at the sink. She had started to undress. I had never seen my mother in only her bra before. For a moment, I forgot fear, and was ashamed.

"What happen?" Michael asked behind me.

She pointed at the toilet. Thick red liquid filled the bowl. Had all that come out of her? How was she still standing up? My dinner threatened to creep up my throat. The thought of spitting into my mother's blood made me swallow it back down.

"Where's it from?" My voice shook.

She pointed at the bathtub. More blood. The tap, still on, gushed red into the tub, splashed it up onto the tiled wall. This was not from my mother. Michael fled. I could feel my mother shaking. I looked up at the ceiling. I expected its ordinary white to comfort me, but it felt like a lie.

In the kitchen, our father was bent over the sink, retching. Beside him was a glass half full of what could have been cherry juice. The five-gallon bottle of drinking water by the fridge was stained the same way. I ran outside and turned on the hose. It stuttered, then gushed. It was as if an enormous vein had been slashed, spraying life into the morning.

∞

It was not only our home; the news told us that. At school the next day, everyone was quiet, keeping fuzzy teeth and night breath private, faces unwashed, underarms sprayed with deodorant but underneath, ripe. That afternoon, the rain, a remnant of the averted storm, fell clear and pooled crimson, as if the earth was contaminated.

Michael said it wasn't blood, it couldn't be because it didn't taste like blood, didn't taste at all. It was simply red, and thicker than water; something like poinciana petals steeped in milk. We now ate off dishes wiped down with rubbing alcohol, and, when that ran out, with Dettol. Even the best meal of macaroni and chicken and broccoli and beets becomes unpalatable when it smells like a nursing home floor.

∞

Water shipped in from Andros began to tinge as it drew near Nassau. The barges stopped coming on Wednesday. Juice and soda, which remained their proper colour, shot up to six dollars a can, then eight dollars. Those who could fled for family islands; the problem had not spread there, though no one could say why.

"Is it Voodoo?" I asked Mummy, as she emptied bottle after bottle of water into the sink. She did not reply. We could hear the TV on in the living room.

"The devastation is unparalleled," the reporter announced. "Hundreds are feared dead and even more missing after freak winter hurricane Raquel made landfall here just yesterday."

My eyes drifted over to the stack of clothes and food on the counter. They seemed as useless as the tainted bottles. What would happen to those people waiting for my old shirts now that we had a disaster of our own? I looked up at Mummy to ask her if church was still having a drive, but her eyes seemed far away. Her hands, mechanical and firm, cracked the seal on another bottle and tipped it upside down. The liquid gurgled, set itself free.

∞

School and work were suspended on Thursday. On Friday, our phone rang. No one answered it. The machine picked it up, and Pastor's voice screeched through the living room, announcing a special emergency service—solace, he said, for the disconcerted.

Daddy pushed his plate away, his bowl of grits untouched. The mush was dense and salty, flecked through with chunks of pallid carrots and beans. "Well, I won't be going. You ask me, that man is where all this trouble started. He see funny things already with that hurricane coming out of nowhere. Instead of trying to lift people up, he pick that time to try turn us against each other?"

"I staying home too." Michael's voice was firm. Was this another strange happening, being able to opt out of church?

"Nobody excused you from worship," Mummy said.

"But in there stuffy, and we ain' even had proper breakfast!"

"Be glad we had food." Mummy got up from the table, even though her plate was still mostly full. "You try making grits with canned soup."

"Should we call Jeanne?" I said, then remembered last Sunday. For a moment, I was back there again, in the world that made sense. I wondered if Daddy was right, if Pastor was somehow to blame for the cursed water. Or was this the fulfillment of Pastor's words? Were we being punished for having bad people, people who did not love God, living amongst us? I looked to Mummy, waiting for her answer. She marched over to the garbage with my father's bowl, stepped on the pedal furiously, and flipped the bowl over. The grits hit the bottom of the can with a purposeful thump.

"They don't even have a phone," Michael muttered, then added, under his breath, "dummy."

∞

Mummy drove us in silence, pulling up outside the pathway that led to Jeanne and Ms. Louise's house. It struck me suddenly: Ms. Louise knew every corner of every cupboard in our kitchen, knew where we kept the good sheets and where we put the old ones. Jeanne rode in our car every week, ate Sunday dinner with us. Yet I did not know the first thing about where they lived—only that they did not have a phone, and that their house was not visible from the street. From where we always dropped them, all I could see was thick greenery—wild trees, shrubs strung over with vines. Mummy shut the engine off. Michael leaned back in his seat.

"I'll go get her." I unlocked my door and climbed out. The path through the grassy overgrowth was surprisingly straight, as though people had spent years walking carefully through the bush, following an invisible line. I saw glimpses of painted clapboard walls and flashes of concrete through the thick. Finally, the greenery opened up to a clearing crammed with small homes. I didn't know if Ms. Louise and Jeanne's house was yellow or green or blue.

A small boy peered out from the doorway of a yellow home.

"You know where Jeanne live?" I asked. He ducked behind the door, then peeped out again, pointing the other way. I retraced my steps "Jeanne?" I called. My voice seemed to come out half-hearted. She could be anywhere. I took a few more steps. The two nearest structures ended abruptly, over before they had begun. They were barely more than shacks. Jeanne couldn't live here. I called her name again. Coming from a light-blue home, a familiar voice raised. Ms. Louise. I heard Jeanne answer, but I couldn't make out her words. Pastor's warning flashed through my mind: *people who-a dabble in the Darkness.* I raised my fist to knock. Another string of chatter from inside, and they both laughed. Bubbling, beautiful, pure. Like water. Suddenly, I did not want to find her. I did not want to knock, to wait while she dressed and put on shoes. I did not want her in our car.

Two honks from the street. We would be late. It felt so natural, so easy, to turn down the path. To walk, quick, through the green. To join my family, alone.

"Well?" Mummy craned her neck to look at me. I focused on buckling my seatbelt. Welcomed the shadows that hid my face.

"She can't come."

∞

Mummy made us sit in the front row, under her scrutinizing eye. The congregation was thin. Some people must have been working; others, perhaps, were too self-conscious to worship unwashed. When we rose to sing, I scoured the sombre faces to see which of the righteous had turned up. Mummy prodded me with her fan's handle until I faced forward.

"The Lord has presented us with a *mighty* trial." The pastor gripped the pulpit, his voice low, as though sharing a secret. "But surely, *surely* we are STRONG! I remark how, just earlier this week, we GATHERED together, close at hand, bringing provisions, and bringing victuals together for our unfortunate neighbours who faced the *wrath* of the storm, amen. Now, our own storm is upon us, brought upon us"—he paused, leaning forward, staring, it seemed straight at me—"by *sin*."

"I need to pee." My whisper came out less than hushed. Mummy frowned slightly and waved me on.

In the hallway, I hesitated outside the kitchen, then stepped inside. The tiles bore a mottled grey design, an accidental splotch near one corner repeated evenly, a hundred ordered mistakes. The water cooler stood in the corner. Someone had removed the large blue bottle that usually sat on top. It had been hidden away, along with the cone-shaped paper cups. I took a step toward the cooler. Its taps beckoned, one blue, one white.

"Brothers, sisters, let us not be taken unawares, for we know that the Day of the Lord shall come upon us like a thief in the night." The volume of the speaker above my head was low, as though it did not want to startle me. "These strange happenings, these, you may say, disasters, give us cause to listen, to look. To examine our own lives. To consider how our own sins may have led to how we are now affected."

I reached forward, extended a finger, my right index one. The plastic of each handle was cool.

"Impacted."

A piece of paper, taped just above the taps, bore a hand-written order: *Do Not Use*. The sign fluttered against the back of my hand.

"Chastised."

I pressed the safety valve. A trickle of red slid out onto the floor. I let go.

"Punished."

I grabbed a handful of paper towels from beside the fridge and squirted dish soap onto them, then scrubbed at the puddle on the floor. At first, I only seemed to be spreading the mess, rubbing it into the tiles, but eventually, it was all but gone. Across the hall, I heard a toilet flushing, and a moment later, a door opening, then falling closed.

"You alright?"

I looked up at Deacon Brown in the doorway and nodded. He smiled and disappeared, the soft creak of his shoes growing quieter until the sound was swallowed up by the pastor's voice. I should get back. Mummy would be wondering where I was. I asked myself how Deacon Brown had cleaned his hands, if he had done so at all, and then, if I would be punished for thinking of what a man of God did in the privacy of the men's room. In the hallway, I pushed the men's room door open, peered in. The place was still and clean. The door swung closed when I let go, quick to hold its secrets.

When I returned to our pew and sat down, Michael glanced at me, then turned away. Droplets of sweat were gathering on his forehead. They glistened; one slid down the bridge of his nose and hung like fresh dew on the tip of a banana leaf. I looked away, fighting the urge to lick my lips. Beside me, my mother shuffled, fanning herself. She nudged Michael. He flinched. The droplet shook loose and landed on the tiles.

"And though we take care not to be *swayed* from our chosen path, flock," the pastor said, his voice far away, as if from across a desert, "we do well to remember—"

The creak, low, slow, long, came sudden. I turned back to see the door to the sanctuary open. The daylight, glaring, fresh, wavered with unseasonable heat, and made indoors seem gloomy. It took me a moment to make out the face of the woman who stood in the gap. I did not know her. She had on a dark skirt with small flowers printed across it, and her head was tied with a yellow scarf. She wore sneakers and had a Big Value bag over one wrist. The lettering was worn off the blue plastic, only a shadow of the shopping-cart logo left behind. She pulled the door shut behind her; it squealed again. She lowered herself into a pew near where Michael, Jeanne and I usually sat.

Mummy's fan handle dug into my side. I straightened up. Behind the pulpit, the pastor swayed. Opened his mouth, but no word came out. He blinked, dazed.

"Pastor ga faint!" someone behind us hissed, and Michael ran over to open the window closest to the front. The pianist sat down hastily and raised an unscheduled song from the side of the stage. The choir scrambled to its feet and joined in. The congregation was reluctant, soft of voice. The pastor sank to his knees . . . Praying? Weak? I could not tell. The music soared, gaining timbre. Deacon Brown appeared holding something draped under a paper towel. He stooped down to the pastor and I saw a whisper pass between them. The pastor pulled the towel away and raised a pointed paper cup to his mouth. I watched the lift and fall of his throat as he swallowed. Once. Twice.

∞

No one spoke on the way home.

"Let's stop by the beach," I said on a whim, because the ocean water was still clear. Mummy swung down onto Prince Charles Drive and followed it to the end. She parked right at the edge of the sea wall.

"Y'all go ahead," Mummy said, cracking her door open.

Michael rolled his window down, but didn't move. I got out of the car. I shed my shoes, then my socks. I tossed them into the back seat.

"Don't get your clothes dirty," Mummy said, listlessly.

I walked past a few parked vehicles. They belonged to others early from church, or people who hadn't gone. The concrete was hot and hard under my arches; the sand offered welcome relief. Closer to the water, the sand grew firm. The tide was neither high nor low, but seemed to be coming in. I could easily see through the few inches to the bottom.

I stepped in. It looked good enough to drink, and it was cool. I wished I could stand there until the sea grew deep enough to immerse me, until I could feel clean again. I walked a little further into the sea. The water lapped at my legs. I wiggled my toes and watched the sand kick up around them.

Then I saw it. Where my skin touched the water, redness was beginning to bleed into the clear. Later, in high school, I would come to see how much this was like getting your period in a pool, seeing red coming out of you, not wanting to believe, swimming away and finding, in horror, that what you fear follows you. I turned toward the shore. I had only taken a few steps into the water—how could the car seem so far away? I tried to shout but my throat was dry.

A girl sat on the sand, barefoot, in the shade of a tree. Her hand settled on the top of a bottle of water, half obscuring it. I licked my lips, tasting salt. I knew something in the twist of her mouth.

"Jeanne?" I called out.

The girl did not answer, did not even flinch. Slowly, she lifted the bottle to her mouth. The liquid was colourless, perfect.

"Jeanne!" I called again, then coughed. My head swam with a rush of understanding: she had seen me outside her house, felt the *bumbumbumbum* of my heart in my chest, smelled the fear prickling under my armpits, seen me turn away.

The girl's eyes shifted to meet mine. She stood up, stepped forward out of the tree's shade. It was not Jeanne after all. It was not even a girl; it was a grown woman, in worn jeans and a sleeveless shirt. I knew her face from somewhere, but I could not say who she was. She smiled, glinting teeth clean and white. I could almost smell the mint on her breath, soap on her skin. She called out, "You thirsty?" Then launched her water bottle high toward me.

As the bottle passed through the air, I saw the water turn—red not there, then everywhere. It hit the sea and went down, sucked into the stain.

I ran, but the water slowed me, and the colour was thickening, following me. I screamed for my mother, for Michael, and the shoreline seemed to grow further away, the red spreading now, lapping up to touch the sand, seeping into the shore. I wanted to shout again, but my throat seemed to be closing in. Couldn't they see I was struggling to reach them? I pushed and pushed for the shore, but it would not come. The redness was spreading further, through the sand, creeping up the concrete steps. They must have been up there in the car, but I could not see their faces through the glare of sun on the glass.

VISITING

MY MOTHER'S FRIENDS ARE ELEGANT BIRDS, each with her own muted plumage—a pale green blouse and blue skirt, a buttery floral dress, tailored pants with a carefully pressed crease down the front of each leg, a linen skirt that stops just below the fullest point on a pair of curved calves. Half-drunk glasses of punch wait on coasters pooled with condensation, melting ice diluting the drinks from pomegranate-red to demure pink. Their conversation rings through the living room, solos and duets here and there, then a frenzied chorus, then harmonies, four or five threads all at once, in different corners between smaller groups, coming together again and then quieting when a captivating story demands attention.

I slip onto the armchair near the hallway. They are only discussing their jobs, and how Mrs. Robinson (who is absent this week) should, in fact, *has to*, do something about that niece she keeps letting come to church in tight little skirts that show all her business. My mother has not looked at me since I sat down. She is pleased for me to listen in, for now, but as soon as voices dip to discuss the confidential, Mummy's eyes will slide over toward me. "Margaret, go check on the laundry," she'll say, and that will be my cue to leave, whether there is laundry on the line or not. After, I can usually manage, at best, to sidle past the living room twice before Mummy will catch my eye and shake her head, lips pressed closed. On the third try, she'll excuse herself to assign me some rare and torturous task. Last month, it was reorganizing the linen closet by colour. Before that, scrubbing the collars on a whole hamper of Daddy's dress shirts.

"I just don't know what to do with him," Ms. Moss says now, setting her glass down empty. "He's been out of work six months. It's like he can't settle down and just look. He'll go out Monday, Tuesday. By Wednesday he's home for lunch thumbing through the wanted ads."

"What's the problem?" Mrs. Smith leans forward, the motion stirring up the Florida Water, alcoholic and medicinal, she always wears. I wrinkle my nose.

"His temper." Ms. Moss shakes her head. "I keep telling him, you can't go on the people job and act like the boss. But he doesn't understand that."

"You know how they are these days, want everything handed to them straight off."

"I don't think that's true." Across the room, Ms. Gardiner, who is young, younger even than Mummy, breaks in. She doesn't speak often, which is a shame. Her voice is a bell. "My granddad was like that. He was in jail seven times, every time for getting in a fight. My grammy says his temper was always hot."

A chorus of *mmmm, that's true* and *yeah* and *some people struggle with that* scatters through the room.

"But I feel it's worse now, somehow." Ms. Moss takes her line up again. "It's not only him, the company he keeps, all these bad friends—"

"Oh, you have to watch that!"

"Mmm, be careful."

"He's how old now?"

"Going on nineteen. His second year out of school, he should have settled into himself by now."

"He doesn't want to pick up a trade?"

"He was supposed to go off to school." Ms. Moss fidgets; talking about her son seems to agitate her, and yet she does, every week, for ten minutes at least. "And then with the problems with his sister, all our savings had to go toward sorting her out . . ."

Shuddering hums vibrate through the room. This is one of the matters I've not been allowed to hear about, so I've had to rely on my imagination. It can't be that Ms. Moss's daughter has merely gotten pregnant; when Mrs. Smith's granddaughter was found to have been five months along, Mummy called me in from the kitchen, where I was pretending to finish my Science project, and had me refill the lemonade glasses so she could be sure I heard about the pitfalls of this destructive path. It couldn't be something to do with extremely bad health—I was allowed to stay when Mrs. Wright talked about her son's weak heart. That, too, had created a convenient frame of reference for Mummy to remind me how grateful I should be for legs I can walk on and arms strong enough to sweep and mop. Ms. Moss's daughter's secret has to be something much more scandalous. I sit very still, hoping she'll elaborate quickly, before Mummy concocts an excuse to usher me from the room.

"Mary, you look weighed down today," Mrs. Smith says to Mrs. Hannah, who leans back in the settee with a weary smile.

"Well, you know what I told you about last week."

"Oh, you mean the—"

Mummy straightens up, ever alert. "Pardon me, ladies. Margaret, those dishes still in the sink?"

"No, Mummy." I suppress a smile. Her cunning has backfired; she set me that task earlier to get me out of the living room so she and Daddy could talk. "And the kitchen counter is clear, the garbage is out, and I finished the laundry."

"You ironed—"

"Daddy's shirts, and my uniforms for next week."

A snicker—I'm sure it's from Ms. Gardiner but I don't dare look over to confirm—is cut short by the narrowing of my mother's eyes.

"I think you need to mop the—"

"I got up early today and mopped the kitchen and the front room. The bathroom too." I had waved a wet piece of paper towel over the tiles, so it isn't a total lie. A tiny muscle in my mother's jaw flinches and I hastily add, "Ma'am."

"Hmph." Mrs. Smith makes a low sound of approval. "I wish my granddaughter would work that hard."

"Indeed." Mummy's smile lasts a moment too long.

"She should stay. When I was her age, I could have learned a lot from big people talk." Ms. Gardiner gives me a warm glance.

"We're all women here," Mrs. Smith agrees. Mrs. Hannah nods. Mummy turns back to Mrs. Hannah. I sit up straight in my chair and allow myself the tiniest grin. I may be the only one who notices the slight purse to my mother's lips as she waits for her friend to continue. My heart flutters a moment; I know I'll pay for this later, but I intend to enjoy myself now.

"Well," Mrs. Hannah resumes, "you know how Jackson is."

A chorus of *mmm hmms*, harmonized.

"I thought you all were going to counselling."

She shakes her head. "We went two, three times. Then the night before our next session, I turn over in the bed, he ain' there. And I finally got confirmation."

"What, someone told you something?"

Mrs. Hannah tugs lightly at her sleeve, brushing off some invisible thing. "Someone called me one afternoon and told me they saw him parked up someplace. With somebody. In our car."

"Yeah, but a lot of people drive that type of truck." Ms. Gardiner tries to sound optimistic.

"I done been through that. The person who tell me, they know it was him. They went over and knocked on the glass."

"What?"

"What he say?"

She leans back into the chair, her arms folded over her chest. Her large frame seems to grow smaller. "What could he say?"

"Maybe they were lying. Who caught him?"

"My brother."

Gasps reverberate around the room.

"Four fifteen on a Tuesday. Big, broad daylight."

"Mmmmph."

Shaking heads.

I think of Mr. Hannah. One of many suited men at church, handing out straw baskets at one end of the pew, collecting them, newly full, at the other. He is tall, his thick stomach restrained by a belt, his thick hair mottled black and grey. He taught me in my fourth year of Bible classes, and now he tutors eight of us in Math after school. He's nice enough, but I can't imagine why anyone would want to go with him if they didn't have to, if their name didn't happen to be Mrs. Hannah.

The women continue talking around me, clucking and sighing. Mrs. Hannah's eyes are dry, but Mummy leans forward to push the box of tissues toward her. Mrs. Hannah obediently takes two, lifting them out of the box quickly so they make a little swish. Even tearless, she looks so sad. I glance away, and my eye meets Ms. Gardiner's. She gives me a mournful little smile. In that moment, the loss seems so much greater than just Mrs. Hannah's. It seems the whole afternoon, the soft fabrics and laughter, the chorus of gossip and gripes, the delicately glazed lemon sponge, will be ruined. I rack my brain for something to say that will lighten the room, that will, at least, make Ms. Gardiner smile again.

Suddenly, I remember.

"Maybe your brother didn't see right," I say. The hush falls over the room in an instant. Mrs. Smith's hand pauses inches away from her lemonade glass. Ms. Gardiner freezes, her arm in mid-air.

"What's that?" Mrs. Hannah looks over at me, her shoulders low. She seems even smaller, now.

Across the room, my mother clears her throat. She leans forward, daring me to open my mouth again. My heart hammers inside my chest. I know I shouldn't really be speaking, should count myself lucky to have been tolerated this far.

"Why you say that?" Mrs. Hannah speaks again. Her eyes search my face as though we've just met.

"Mr. Hannah always teaches Advanced Math after school." My words burble out before I can arrange them. "And he gives my friend a ride home 'cause her mother has to work late."

Mummy leans forward so far she seems about to rise out of her chair. "Margaret, go to your room."

"Let her speak." Mrs. Hannah holds up a hand. "Which friend?"

I glance over at Mummy for help. Her head is bent down, as if she has skipped forward to the evening and is sitting alone in her yellow housecoat and slippers, reflecting on the day.

"Corrine." I feel like a traitor, without quite knowing why. "But he couldn't have been doing anything bad, Mrs. Hannah, because he was dropping off Corrine, and she's the same age as me, she ga be thirteen this summer—"

"More punch!" Mummy is up on her feet, moving fast out of the room, gathering up my glass, her glass.

In the kitchen, the sound of the fridge door opening, closing, ice clinking. In the living room, silence settles. Mrs. Rolle stares intently at the spot on the floor where her granddaughter spilled her drink last week before I was made to take her outside to play. Ms. Gardiner is shaking her head again and again. Mrs. Hannah sits, frozen, angry, and something else, some emotion I can't name. I long to be stringing clothing up on the line, scrubbing the grout between the kitchen tiles, rearranging the cleaning products under the bathroom sink, but my body feels frozen in its place. The silence around us is even thicker now. I stare down at the polka dots on my skirt. My arms are goose-pimpled, the fine hairs are alert. I am part of it, now.

A BOND UNSEEN

MALCOLM'S SHOE

THEY CAME IN THE MIDDLE OF THE NIGHT, fists on the wooden front door, beating till it rattled in its frame. Mummy crawled into my room like a baby, pulled me out of the bed onto the floor, her hand clapped over my mouth, though I didn't need it, no way was I going to scream, to speak, to even gasp. Shoved me under the bed, the tiles cold. Dusty down there and hard to breathe. She rolled her body, a barrier between me and whatever might come. The fists getting louder. Was it two, three guys, seven? Feet rustling through the grass below my window, voices calling, "Hey, come out here, boy, we know you in there, you better bring your ass out here, better hurry up." From Malcom's room, nothing. I wondered if Mummy had hidden him someplace, shoved him under his own bed, crumpled him into the closet, a pillow jammed in his mouth. Then his voice breaking loose from inside his room, curling out.

"What y'all want?"

"Boy, you know what we want. Where the thing?"

"I ain' know what y'all talkin' bout. Come out my mummy yard."

Then the sound of something hard thudding against the window panes. "We ain' goin' nowhere. You come out here. Or you want us come in there?" There was a bang, a tremendous thud, like a body, a living body, a body tight with anger, throwing itself against the door. The house shook.

"Get out my yard. I callin' the police on you."

The door thudded again, heavier this time. I squeezed my eyes shut, struggling for air. Mummy's nails dug into my shoulder. A third thud. And then a crash, glass breaking. I bit down on my hand to keep my scream in. Squeak of tennis shoes on tiles, down the hall, to the kitchen. Then the slow click of the locks on the kitchen door. The bolts drawn. They were expecting Malcolm at the front, wouldn't know he had made it to the back side of the house.

"Don't go out there!" Mummy shouted, throwing her voice after him.

And then they were upon him. Thick voices and pounding fists landing, shoes hammering the ground, and Malcolm's voice, twisted like a bedsheet pulled loose from a clothesline and wrapped strangely, wrapped wrong, around a tree branch. And Mummy's wailing long and loose, flapping free. Then it stopped. Footsteps pulling away, the voices hushed. The opening of car doors, engines starting, then drifting away. Mummy's wailing began to slow, the windstorm that had caught it settling down until it lay limp.

My face was wet. I freed myself from my mother, crawled out the other side of the bed, jostling two old books, a lost toy out of my way. Mummy let out a last, shuddering cry that crashed through the room in waves. And then silence.

I turned on every light I could to scare the fear away. The hallway light, shining into Malcolm's room, the bed unmade but nothing else in disarray, his boy smell, sweat and salt and stale socks and heavy cologne and a slight, almost hidden whiff of smoke, drifting out. The living room, everything in its proper place, the picture of Grammy on the wall next to Grampy's, even though they hadn't slept in the same bed in years, the carpets clean, the curtains still drawn tight against the night's dark. The dining room, chairs tucked in, table cleared of last night's dishes. And the front door still now in its frame, the chain on.

I turned on the kitchen light, yellow spilling over the cupboards, the fridge, the counter, tidy and neat. Malcolm's smell in here too, musky with sleep. And the back door, shut. I pulled it. It was locked.

My fingers shaking, I fumbled with the lock, its metal slick and cold. The door stuck, reluctant to give in. I pulled harder and it gave way with a creak.

The yard was lit in flickering white. This gave me comfort. Nothing bad happens with the outside light on.

"Hey, Malcolm?" Barefoot, I stepped out, the concrete patio, the cold grass, the guava tree's leaves reaching down to brush my arm.

"Malcolm?"

The grass was matted down. Here, there, splashed with red wet. *No.*

"Malcolm?" My voice came out tight, high.

I saw his shoe. I recognized it, a white and red sneaker, on its side in the grass, loosely laced, never tied. I turned it over. Size eleven. It was his.

And then a rustle from the back of the yard and I grabbed it, this part of Malcolm, and ran for the door, slammed and locked it behind me. Through the door, then, the small call of a bird, confused, crying dawn in the thick of night.

I cradled the shoe like a doll. I took it to his room. Mummy had woken her voice again. "My baby," she called from under the bed. "My one baby, my one good son, my first, my boy. Oh, Lord Jesus. Oh, they take him. Oh, Malcolm, where you gone?"

∞

The telephone rings at dawn. I pick it up. "Hello?"

"Yes, Mrs. Dean, please." A woman's voice, polite and calm.

"She can't talk right now."

"This her daughter?"

Should I say? What if it's someone bad?

"Who's this?" I ask.

"I'm calling from the police station. Is there a grown-up I can talk to?"

Mummy has come out from under the bed. She lies on mine, the sheet over her from head to toe. She won't move.

"No," I say.

"I need to talk to your mother. She isn't there?" Then, when I say nothing, "Well, when she wakes up, you tell her to call Blue Hill Road police station, you hear? You understand me?"

"Yes, ma'am."

∞

When the sky has opened up, we drive down together. Mummy has put on her good clothes, her peach blouse and her navy-blue skirt, a pair of high-heeled shoes.

"I come for my son. Malcolm Augustus Dean."

The face of the policeman at the front desk is unreadable. I stick tight to Mummy's side.

"The little girl can't come in. How old is she?"

"She nine, and you out your mind if you think I'm leaving my one good child out here by herself."

The policeman shakes his head, and I first think he means no, but he means *whatever, I don't care to argue,* because he gets up and pushes open a door that leads deep into a hallway, and we go in. I have Malcolm's one shoe to give to him, hidden in my backpack. I swing the bag to my side and reach inside, close my fingers around the smooth laces. New, still clean.

"He's in there." The policeman stands outside the door, holding it open. Mummy starts inside. Something holds me back. The hallway is cool, smells of sweat and something else. I can't see into the room properly—only fluorescent lights, a bare wall—but I know if I go in there, I won't come out the same.

"Yes, you come in, baby, I want you see just how people do your brother. I want you see for yourself." Her voice is smooth, as though she has ironed out all last night's crumple and loose. I know the policeman is lying, Malcolm isn't inside, not really, but Mummy is so sure, so calm, and I don't want to see, and I do. I step forward with her.

And then we both see. Mummy gasps and turns me, pressing my face into her side. All I see after that is the back of my eyelids.

∞

At the front desk, Mummy scratches pen over paper. I can hear it, but I keep my face up against her side. Finally, I open my eyes but turn them to the floor, my forehead still nestled against her. The tiles are old and cream, scratched with the years but so recently mopped the streaks are visible still. I focus on those streaks, traces of a careless mop dragged this way then that.

Then we're outside, at the car. The sky is cheerful and blue, and someone laughs as they ride by, the bike's squeak a traitorous song. Mummy lets me stand there, still plastered to her, small breeze moving around us. I hear her rustle in her bag, the sound muffled. I am not outside. Malcolm is not in there. Malcolm is standing with us, his face twisted in a naughty grin, his head hung down, eyes up, mischief made. He is getting in the front seat, shoving me toward the back, *You think you's big people, eh?*

He is not stretched out on that table, flat, one eye moulded shut, his jeans ripped. And his feet turned straight up in the air. Two tennis, red and white. His size elevens, right there.

"Come," Mummy says. "We have to go up to the morgue now. They're taking him there. You understand?" The parking lot is empty, only Mummy, only me. She peels me from her side. "You have to be grown now. I can't baby you."

I sit in the front seat, the backpack at my feet. Nassau passes us. Clean morning light, bundles of children shuffling along to school late, each unique in their matching uniforms, green skirts, white blouses, black shoes. Tall, short, fat, skinny, jostling each other. I watch them pass. Cars, all different colours, a bus, its horn quick and privileged, as it swings out into traffic, not a care. Big trees, and boys, men, one walking alone, another two sitting on a wall, one shovelling food into his mouth from a small white container. Clunky sneakers, loosely laced, rising up to meet the bottoms of his jeans.

The hospital is drawing near. Big silk cotton trees, roots as tall as a man, flank the street, shade spilling out all around.

"Mummy, what will they do with his clothes?" I ask, my voice breaking something thick in the car.

She says nothing. I ask again.

"His clothes?" She looks over at me, losing focus on the road and getting too close to the car in front. "I don't know what they do with the clothes. I guess they give them to us. I don't want them." Her voice breaks. "I want *him*."

We pull into the parking lot. I want to stay in the car, but she makes me get out. "I'm not leaving you anywhere, anything could happen. You see that now, right? You see that now." She glances down at the bag. "What you have in there anyway?"

"Something I had brought for Malcolm."

She pulls the backpack from me, reaches in.

"What is this? His shoe?" She shakes her head, her eyes starting to wet. She pushes it back into my hands as she walks away, toward the entrance.

When she speaks again, her voice is new and hard. "Well, he ain' ga need that anymore."

I open my mouth, I want to tell her he was wearing both his shoes, but she carries on, harder still.

"I ain' know what the hell you bring that here for." We are at the bottom of the stairs, a rusted green trash can behind me. She snatches the shoe out of my hands, shoves it into the garbage. Then we are walking up the steps, pushing the glass door open, going through the metal detector, security searching Mummy's bag.

"You know your daughter crying," the security guard says, as though I am not there.

"Of course she crying, you know what they did to her brother? You'll read about it in the paper, anyway. Malcolm Augustus Dean."

And we walk through the halls, passing people, some faces long, others laughing, wishing good mornings Mummy doesn't return. We walk away, away from the third shoe, in his size, spattered with his blood. We walk toward the morgue, neither of us touching.

PLANTING SEASON

THE CRUCIFERS SPROUT DAYS AFTER I scatter seeds. They send up diligent leaves and produce tiny, tight crowns. I walk through the rows each morning to check their growth. My crop is so robust that butterflies come in advance of flowers. The white-winged visitors are simple and small. They flutter around my head, reassuring, homely, communing with me as they land, rest, rise again.

Disaster strikes overnight. I step outside, work shoes on, bag on my shoulder, and meet skeletonized plants, broccoli heads ghoulishly bulbous atop scrawny stems. The leaves have been devoured. I lay the fist-sized heads on the roof of my car, then, in my silk blouse and pencil skirt and red heels, pull up the ruined crop.

∞

Joanne appears at my desk at a quarter to twelve, a stack of this morning's newspapers in her arms, the emergency lights casting a white haze over her.

"What you working on?"

"Waiting for someone to call me back. Can't do much with the power off." I slip my left pump back on, hoping she hasn't noticed the blackened sole of my foot. "You need me to do something?"

"Meeting in my office."

I follow Joanne down the hallway. Just before I reach her door, Leonard steps out from behind a cabinet and we nearly collide.

"Sorry!" I say, veering out of his way. He sidesteps me, holding tight to three packs of printer paper.

"Nice skirt." The words are a stroke up my spine. Before I can speak, he dips, and fingers brush the inside of my left ankle. Leonard straightens up, holds up his hand to show me the smudge of dirt. He smirks like his mouth is full of something sweet. I keep moving, don't answer, but I feel flushed with the memory of touch on my skin.

Half the female population of the newsroom is crowded into Joanne's workspace, pizza boxes open, shoes kicked off. Outside the window, a light drizzle falls over the parking lot. I squeeze in beside Elaine and help myself to a slice.

"Weather like this," Rhonda grumbles, "I business snuggle up with my boo."

"Ya know?" Tanya passes me a cup of ginger ale. I don't, so I say nothing.

"You know how much baby we ga see in one good nine months?"

"Elaine gettin' tears in her eye." Joanne nudges her.

"Please. I need a night off." Elaine bites into a hunk of garlic bread. "You know how tired I is? Every damn night, dread."

"You complainin'? Some people don't see none in a year!"

"Chile, I's don get tired." Rhonda snorts. "That's my hour and a half a cardio a day, if I don' get that I's don' exercise."

"Hour and a half, eh?"

"Who have time for that? Twenty minutes, I good, girl. Let me get my beauty rest, please."

I pick the olives off my pizza, thankful for the flurry of attention directed away from me. As Symonne demonstrates the best of her new moves, most of which seem to be named after safari animals, my mind wanders.

I am sixteen, in my mother's kitchen. Vegetables lie in the sink, the soup pot steaming up the room. Mummy sets a cutting board on the counter a little too heavily, bangs the spice cupboard open, slams it shut. We scrub potato skins and carrots in silence.

"You gettin' older now, Kendra." She slips off a garlic clove's thin wrapping. "You behaving?"

Her words surprise me. I'd assumed she was mad at Mr. Grey, who hasn't been by the house in four days. How is this about me? I get straight As at school, have never had so much as a detention. I slice a lime cleanly. "Yes, ma'am."

"Better be. I don't want you making silly mistakes. Don't need history to repeat itself." She snatches a potato out of the sink, thumps it onto the cutting board, and hacks it in two. I stay silent; when she's in these moods, it's better to lay low, to listen without inquiry. Half the time she's venting more than scolding, anyway. Minutes pass before she speaks again. "And when you do decide to start—you know—don't be stupid. Don't let just anyone up in your business."

"Business?" I fish the last lime seed out of the measuring cup, waiting for her to elaborate.

She tosses the potato into the pot, sending water dancing out onto the burner, sizzling, vexed. "Just be careful. Some men," she hisses, "ain' no better than dogs."

I'd feigned a cut finger and fled the scene. Now, I wished I had stayed. Listened. Learned.

"You quiet over here, Kendra." Rhonda turns to me abruptly. "What about you and that little hottie you have coming to pick you up for lunch every Thursday?"

"Vince?" Heat washes over me. "He's just a friend." Elaine looks unconvinced and Joanne snorts.

"Let me tell you what that man did on the weekend," Joanne says. On another day, they might pry, but today, appetites whet for sizzle and juice, I'm dropped.

∞

"They ate everything?" My mother sounds like she has never heard of such gross mismanagement.

"I got the top part, but the leaves were all chewed."

"Probably butterflies."

I look out at the cleared patch, betrayed. "I saw some a week or so ago. I thought they were pollinating."

A snicker on the other end of the line. "Pollinating what? Nothing in bloom. Anyway, whatever else they do, butterflies lay eggs that hatch into caterpillars. And caterpillars only have one job, to eat. I thought you knew that."

I can see the accompanying smirk. I drain the blanched florets and dump them into a bowl. "Guess you didn't teach me."

"Well, make sure you check the broccoli before you eat it. Once you see the plant's been chewed, they might be hiding anywhere."

I pick up the dish. The vegetables are bright green against the yellow stoneware. Then I see the curved bodies, pale, tiny legs still. I groan, then hate myself for letting my mother hear it.

"Found 'em?"

"Yup." I open the trash and pour my failure in. "I have to go, Vincent's coming in half an hour."

"You didn't throw it away, did you?"

"Mummy. I'm not serving him steamed worms."

"Caterpillars. Your grammy used to just pick them out. I don't know if your grandfather even knew how much extra protein he got at our table. Tasted good too."

"Wonderful. Well, I found some wild callaloo yesterday. I'll sauté that instead."

"Taking it off the stem?"

"No."

"Hmph," she says, as though washing her hands of an immoral decision.

I turn on the tap, run it cold. "I need to scrub the potatoes."

"You pulled them already?"

"I wanted them small."

"Should have cooked those before your veg."

I bite my bottom lip, drop the potatoes into the sink. Something hits with a heavy clunk.

"What you doing in that kitchen, girl?"

I run water over the harvest and find the culprit, flat and smooth. A perfect brown stone gleams up from the sink.

"Got a rock by mistake?" my mother asks. Of course she knows. A woman should.

∞

Later, I curl on the sofa beside Vince. Our bodies touch, shoulder to shoulder, leg to leg. Is it romantic or simple sense, a natural easing of tired bodies?

"What you think about the garden?" I ask.

He looks toward the window, the drapes still parted, and my heart skips. *Don't get up,* I will him. He thinks for several moments, shifts. Only our knees touch, now.

"You took out some of the greens."

"That's it?" I stretch, hoping it seems natural as my thigh eases against his once again. "I want to know what you *think*! Does it look good?"

He glances over at the table, still littered with the leftovers. "You fishing for compliments?"

"Do I have to fish?"

He settles back, his arm against mine, firm, soft with hair. "You should fence in the yard if you plan on growin' food."

"I spend half the day in an office, wearing too-tight shoes. When I come home, I like feeling free."

"So, buy better shoes. Anyway, dogs come in the yard."

"Let them come, God put them here too, ya know."

"Arrite then. Eat dog piss if you want, but I ain' touchin' ya food." He settles back into the couch, glances over at me. "What you smilin' about?"

"Nothing. Just remembering what we had for dinner."

"What?"

"Garden greens."

He grabs a cushion and bats at me with it. I swipe it away and retaliate. Then he's tickling me and my thoughts turn yellow, laughter and free.

∞

Promptly at eleven, Vince glances at the clock. "Baby, I gone 'fore it get too late," he says. I sit up on the couch, turn the TV off.

"Oh. Okay." The words I want to say stay tucked in my cheek. *You don't wanna stay?*

"I had a good time." He kisses me twice. At the car, he waves. From the window, I wave back.

After he has left, I scrape the leftovers into the garbage. The wilted callaloo regards me from amongst the refuse, my failure highlighted, grassy and glistening. I scour the pot I cooked it in until it shines. Then I begin on the potato pot. After that, I open the cupboard above the stove and examine my saucepans, select the largest and begin to scrub.

"Looks like we won't eat sweet potato from the garden this year." Grammy tosses the yam into her wheelbarrow, then reaches for me. I brace myself for the grip of her hand on my shoulder. She eases herself upright and dusts off her knees. Her tight fingers leave a phantom in my flesh.

"Can't we cut the bad parts off?" I look at the heap of lumps she's pulled up, tangled in the desiccated vines that sprawl and twirl over a third of her land, threatening to claim every inch of earth, vacant and occupied, for themselves.

"Not with weevils all through them." She picks up a tuber, half-eaten. The flesh is alive with white grubs. Grammy tosses it back in the barrow. "Can't salvage anything from them and can't mulch 'em. It has to be burned."

I feel the first prick of tears. "All that time waiting for them to grow, and we get nothing."

Grammy bends to slap at her ankle, warding off a mosquito, then looks me in the eye. "You can't take nature personally." She grabs the wheelbarrow's handles, pushing her loss to the far corner of her plot. Her back is straight, her limbs and body thin. She dumps the load, then abandons the wheelbarrow and marches through the remaining vegetable rows. Grammy stoops, then straightens up, the whole truth of a beet in one hand, rattail root-tip to broad leaves, veined red. "Look," she calls, "these clean!" She has already moved on. But I can't move my feet from the spoiled earth. I feel I will have to stand here forever, mourning our loss until it becomes one with me, until weevil grubs bore through my soles.

I think about the year Grammy stopped growing potatoes as I make the cookware gleam like a smooth-talker's teeth. Think of it an hour later, as I smear the contents of an aloe leaf over my fingertips, red and scored from steel wool. I can hear my mother saying, *Why you ain' put on gloves?* Later, after I dry my hands off and stain the pale blue cloth with aloe juice, she adds, *You ain' know better than that?*

∞

Joanne and I wait for our lunch on a pair of stools in the café across from the newspaper. I turn the salt shaker on its side so the grains slip aside to reveal translucent rice.

The shift of tiny things into new places is soothing. No matter how much I roll it, the salt finds level, rest.

"How's Vince?"

I look up to see Joanne studying me over her half-empty bottle of iced tea.

"He's okay."

"That salt begs to differ. What's goin' on?"

I stand the shaker up and push it away. The restaurant is empty aside from us, it's only half past eleven. Joanne watches a young woman walk by outside in a clingy blue dress, phone raised to her ear. She wears gold extensions that stop just where her round body nips in. Fake nails, bright orange, three inches long, curl from her fingertips into the air, promoting her doctrine of curves. Outside, two men leaning against a work truck follow her with their eyes as she walks, heads turning together.

"Think her dress tight enough?" Joanne sips, then releases her straw. "Talk to me. I promise you, not a problem in this world I haven't been through already. Not when it comes to guys."

"What you makin' all that noise for already?" Leonard had said, the first time. I'd almost asked Joanne and Elaine my questions back then, when I stumbled into work slightly late from lunch, neck cricked, sweaty with guilt. How long do you have to bite the insides of your cheeks to stay quiet? Do other women get flashes of pain in their foreheads and, panting, push the guy away? Do they sometimes feel

a wave of softness, sometimes a band of disgust in their bellies, at him, at themselves? I've had these questions. But I always stop short.

My boss fixes her gaze on me, all girlfriend now, waiting.

"So Vincent . . . he always goes home right when it's—I don't know. When it could start to get . . . serious, I guess."

Joanne studies the scene outside. The woman stands by the bus stop, scrounging shade from a spindly tree. The men have lost interest, returned to their half-dug hole.

"Y'all ever do the do?"

"Of course."

"How many times?"

I freeze, unprepared to create such an elaborate lie. Joanne rolls her eyes.

"He cheatin'." She doesn't bother to lower her voice. "How long y'all been together?"

"We've been hanging out, I don't know. Six months?"

"Dump him. What about your friend from accounting? Leonard?"

"I told you we broke up last summer."

"Yeah, well. I didn't hear you complaining then. You should go back to him."

But Vince does not cheat. An unfaithful man leaves a trail each time, and Vince has nothing to hide. He never has other calls, leaves his phone when he goes to the bathroom. Never smells suspicious, comes by every other evening. Only stays till the night grows suggestively long, then, suddenly, goes, as if someone—a lost shadow left behind by Leonard, perhaps—has whispered to him that this, that I, am not a good idea. I run my tongue over the raised ridges on the insides of my cheeks and reach for the salt shaker again.

∞

"How's Vincent?" my grandmother always asks at what has become the appointed time during Sunday brunch—when everyone has finished their first plates of food and the conversation has hit a comfortable lull.

"Good," I say.

"You happy?" She takes a second helping of my pesto pasta, and the greens.

"Yes, Grammy."

"When y'all gettin' married, now?"

"Mummy, leave the girl alone." My mother holds her hand out and my sister passes her the carrots.

"Jus make sure he don' get too many samples of that pie now, or he ain' ga wan' pay for the rest of the pan," my grandmother says. My sister pushes her chair back and heads to the kitchen. Across from me, Aunt Mildred snorts into her glass.

"You know bout that, right, Mum?" she says, setting it down.

"You got something to say, Mildred?" Grammy looks up from her half-empty plate. "Go ahead. Since you's woman. Backtalk your own mother."

"Y'all saw the news last night?" Uncle Tony shifts in his seat. "Gas prices gone up again." Beside him, his wife keeps her eyes on her plate.

"Come, help Elisha pour water for the table." Mummy aims the order at me as she pushes her chair back and heads for the safety of the kitchen. She is offering me a lifeline, but something keeps me in my seat, gaze on Aunt Mildred, the whites of her eyes tinged pink.

"Remember the time"—Aunt Mildred leans across toward my uncle—"Daddy wife came looking for him and Mum chase her off the porch with a cutlass?"

Uncle Tony looks at Grammy. My grandmother's face is calm.

"Once, the wife threw red paint on the front of the house and Daddy repainted it six times. Six coat of paint and the stain still showed. You believe that?" Aunt Mildred lifts her glass to her mouth again. "End up painting the whole front of the house bright red. Remember that, Barbra?" She turns, throwing her voice into the kitchen. "All the neighbours couldn't stop talking. Mrs. Gardiner used to say you can't hide whore with eggshell white."

"Millie!" my mother hisses from the doorway. "Stop it! Just stop!" In her chair at the head of the table, Grammy leans back, her eyes shut now. She looks like she could be asleep, except for her jaw. She holds it funny, jutting out.

"When Daddy died, the car broke down and we all had to walk half an hour to the church." Aunt Millie's voice is low, calm, as though she's spent all of her anger, now. "Reach there dusty and sweaty ten minutes into the service. And Mum stand up tall at the doorway, in the middle of 'Great Is Thy Faithfulness,' and push past the yellow rope holding the first three pews for family. Sat down right behind the wife and her two children. Big and brisk, say, 'We're family too.'"

Silence settles. Aunt Mildred stares at her half-empty glass. I want to reach across my mother's empty space to touch my grandmother's hand, squeeze her thick, rough fingers.

"Grammy?" My sister's voice comes from the kitchen doorway, behind me. Then she closes the space, envelops Grammy in a hug.

"It's okay, darlin'." Grammy's voice is even. "Your auntie had a little too much to drink. Why don't you bring out that dessert?"

"Tell them, Barb!" Aunt Mildred springs back to life. "You remember. Tell the girls. That was the day you came to the Lord." She leans in, locking eyes with me. I can't help but look back. "We never went to church before, you know. Not Priscilla Francis and her children. Everybody know she was a sinner."

"Mildred, come on." Uncle Tony shakes his head. "Have some respect."

"Don't act like you forget. You girls shoulda been there. Me and Tony were like fish out of water, but your mummy was born for that day. Had on a little lilac dress and a white hat and she sat up with her back straight as a ruler, and no one could tell her she didn't belong. She was right back the next Sunday, and singing in the choir from when she was nine. Sang at Daddy's wife's funeral, too. That's revenge, ay?" She laughs, sour and sharp. "Dressed up like faith, hey, Barbra? You was pious from then, and yet now you got two children with somebody else's man. Like mother, like dau—"

"Enough." Mummy snatches Aunt Millie's beer away and disappears into the kitchen. A second later, the crash of glass against the sink. Aunt Millie stares after her, a half smile shaping her lips into a boomerang.

"Careful, Mildred." Grammy puts her knife and fork together on her plate, pushed up against her uneaten pasta. "Your nieces soon overtake you. Before you know, both of them ga be married and too busy for Sunday brunches, and the only person you'll be stuck in this house with is me. Me and those old stories you love to dig up."

"Time for dessert," Mummy says, authority in her voice, and sets down my sister's creation—round glass dish, fluted pastry shell, orange-brown filling topped with piped cream. I avert my gaze from the pumpkin pie. Of all the weeks for my sister to have strayed from her parade of strudels, eclairs, crepes, macaroons.

My sister comes out with a silver slicer. "Winter squash *cheesecake*," she says firmly, and not even Aunt Millie dares venture a wisecrack. In the silence, Elisha slices through the dessert, metal gliding through soft, coming to rest against the crystal plate with a crisp, warning clink.

∞

After the dishes are done, we prepare to part ways, my sister to her fiancé's house, Mummy to evening prayers. Uncle Tony and his wife take their half-eaten slices home in foil, Aunt Mildred retreats to her room like a sullen teenager.

"You," and Grammy takes hold of my wrist, "I need some help with my chores. Stay behind and help me for a couple minutes."

As the cars pull out of the driveway, their familiar sounds growing faint, Grammy directs me to her basket of clean laundry. Sun comes in through the glass kitchen door, turning our skin to gold as we smooth creases out of blouses, t-shirts.

"How's my girl doing?" she asks. "Really?"

I attempt to fold up a pair of underpants without examining them too closely. The elastic is so exhausted they must stay up with safety pins and pure faith.

"I'm fine, Grammy. How are you? You okay?"

She waves a hand, dismissing the last of my aunt's insults like they're flimsy cobweb threads. "That's just your aunt. I don't know why she felt she had to say it, but she didn't lie. Your mother and Tony don't like to talk about these things, but it doesn't bother me."

I reach for a pair of shorts and push the pockets back into place. "I should have said something."

Grammy chuckles. "I can handle Mildred. She's been my child for most of my life."

"I'm sorry she upset you."

"I'm not upset. She's an honest drunk, at least. More than anything, I was annoyed. That wasn't what I wanted to talk about over dinner."

"What did you want to talk about?"

"That young man of yours. We still haven't met him."

"It's not like that, Grammy."

"What you mean it's not? From what your mother say, he's in your house almost every evening. If it's not serious, must be for fun?" The question rolls off her tongue.

I look over at her. Her back is curved like a tree grown to bend with the wind as she stacks a faded hand towel onto its mate. Her silvered hair is cut short to the scalp, her long, thin fingers now efficiently working a pair of socks into one another, tucking and folding. She lifts her eyes to meet mine, a smile tilting her lips.

"You know," she says, as though I require clarification, "for the pie?"

"Grammy!"

The smile lingers. "We grown. We can't talk?" Behind her, the sun illuminates her hair, silver to bronze.

How did she even get here, sitting tall through insults, shrugging off the recounting of her indiscretions in front of her granddaughters? Not even counting them indiscretions. Now quizzing me about things I can't fix my own mouth to ask. I dip my hand back into the clothes, and my fingers close around something slippery, smooth. I bring my hand back up. Slick, black. Boxer shorts. A man's. "Oh!"

She lifts them out of my hands easily and folds them on her lap, tucking them to the side. "Those are just a friend's."

"A friend's?"

She doesn't reply but she smiles, sly, small. We move through the rest of the clothes and she chats on about politics, about the upcoming storm season, about the price of flour at the organic market downtown. The sun dips. I get my bag and my keys, and hug her at the door.

She closes her fingers around my wrists and pulls me in. I think she wants to give me another hug.

"The last two years," she whispers, "we was never like man and wife. We would share a bed and hold each other. Just doze and talk secrets till dawn."

I open my mouth, wanting the right words to come, questions that will elongate this confession, a sea-glass secret of my own, pale and washed smooth with turning over, with time.

"I surely missed that pie, though." She lets my wrists go and pats my cheek. "Make sure bring that pasta next week. Ya season that up real nice."

I smile. "Yes, Grammy. I will."

∞

When he touches my arm, I melt. An embrace—my chin to his shoulder, his hands on my waist, his back curled to ease my reach. We hold each other, heartbeats doubled, one on each side of our chests. He glances up at the clock. My eyes follow. 10:53. I pull him closer.

"What is it?" he asks, easing away, tucking his shirt in.

There's a space for me to say the words. It stretches out before me, the way potholed, blurred by heat.

He slips his shoes on. "Kenny? What?" Eyebrows a question, hand on the door.

I stand, barefoot, beside him. What do I say next? What do I do? I should know. I should.

PRINCESS

WE LEFT LATE, AFTER MUMMY HAD fallen asleep, the baritone growl of her snore ringing in our ears like an alarm clock.

"I tellin'," Tamika had whimpered from her side of the room. She was dour that we were leaving, not taking her along with us.

"How you ga tell anything after I rip out your tongue?" Gina had held her face so close to Tamika's our little sister could smell her perfume and toothpaste.

"You can't do me nothin', what if I scream?"

Gina held up Tamika's favourite doll. It was twelve or so inches high, with a waist just slightly thicker than its neck. A smile was painted onto its face, fixed in unblinking delight. Tamika had named it Princess.

"You want Princess to come back in one piece?" Gina dangled Princess above the garbage bin by her hair.

Tamika nodded her head, eyes wide with dread.

"Then keep ya mouth shut."

Tamika began to weep, a low, whinnying sound. Her eyes turned to me, pleading for help. I shrugged. I didn't like to torture her, but there was little I could do. Tamika lunged for the doll, and Gina lifted it out of her reach. She swept a pair of scissors off her dresser and opened them menacingly.

"Princess might not even make it out the house in one piece."

Tamika bit her lip, muffling her cry.

"That's better." Gina stuffed Princess into her slim handbag and zipped it closed. A single foot, frozen in the shape of a high heel, protruded from the bag. Tamika shrank back down on her bed. Gina cracked the door open, listening. Clutching the bag to her chest, she picked up her shoes and I grabbed mine. Together, we tiptoed past Mummy's room to the front door.

Outside, we moved down the driveway in our bare feet, careful, slow, as though at any moment we might be caught, called back, our adventure cut short. When we were out of earshot, we burst into giggles that lifted into the night like butterflies bottled up too long.

"What you bringin' that doll with us for?" I said. The night was clear and warm, with just enough breeze to feel free in. Already, the dank silence of our sleeping house seemed worlds away.

"That's our good luck charm."

"That's ransom."

"Well, where I supposed to leave it?" She glanced around for safe areas. "What about in the back of Dino's truck?"

Dino and his father, Mr. Adderley, lived across and down one house from ours. Mr. Adderley was old; we only saw him every once in a while when he came out to cut his lawn, which he invariably did with no shirt on. If we called to him, he would wave back, a quick, deliberate hail, before returning to his chore. Dino, we saw frequently, coming and going. His truck was shiny and black, and he took pride in washing it every Sunday. He always had on shades, so his expression could not be read.

"No, man." The thought of Dino somehow happening upon the doll made me giggle. The sound came out too loud and I clapped my hand over my mouth.

"What? It's *Saturday*, you know what that means."

Every Saturday, Dino's girlfriend came over. On occasion, if one were in the kitchen getting water late at night, or going to pee, the night air would bring in the sounds Dino's girlfriend made.

"Alright, Princess, looks like you ridin' with the big girls tonight!" Gina patted her bag. "Speaking of which. The taxi ga be there for us, right?"

"Of course." My task had been to call the cab driver, which I had done after dinner that evening while Mummy was in the tub. I'd worried the voice on the other end would call me out. "How old you is?" she might say, or "This ain' Mrs. Newburn child callin' for a cab in the night, eh?" I could see her: short and very heavy, breasts large and formed into a single stern ridge. She would be dumplinged into a chair behind a desk, and her mouth would turn down ever so slightly, even when she was not displeased.

"Pick-up from where?" she'd said instead.

I'd given the intersection we were using, two corners up, on the main road and across from the food store, where a streetlight offered a safe place to wait.

"And where you goin'?"

"Club 81."

There was a pause. I held my breath, waiting for her to demand to know my date of birth.

"A driver will be there in forty-five," she said instead.

"I could have someone there for quarter to twelve?"

The woman let out a meaty sigh, as though she was being made to stand up from a comfortable seat.

"Hold on."

I waited, half listening for the sound of the bathroom door opening. Gina glanced over at me from the drainer, where she was unloading clean plates in a lean-to stack.

"Driver 187 ga be there eleven forty-five, ma'am."

I told Gina what the woman had said and she teased me over it as we took the garbage out. "Ma'am. You get a ma'am. You mussee put on your Mummy voice."

"What Mummy voice?" I pretended not to understand.

"You know what I mean." She had lifted her chin, eyes at haughty half-mast. *"Yes, good evening, I am calling for a very important purpose, thank you."*

Now, we slipped our shoes on and began to walk faster, arm in arm, down the road. We had never been out this late on our own before. The air was quieter and somehow more alive, as though it was made up of billions of tiny breathing things beating their wings, urging us forward. Our shoes slowed us down. Gina's were ones she had bought and hidden away at the back of our closet, thrilling blue heels, viciously pointed at the tip. They made her bare legs seem inches longer than usual, made her walk with a swish that bounced her bottom and fluttered the folds of her dress. I had borrowed an old pair of Mummy's. They were considerably less thrilling, but were black and shiny, and anyway I had on jeans, so they were less important. They fit better than I had expected; I had thought my feet were smaller than Mummy's and had stuffed the toes with cotton, which I was now regretting. I'd take it out when we got into the cab.

At the intersection, the street was busier. A few cars flew by us. We scanned the area, then saw our cab waiting for us in the supermarket parking lot. We crossed the road.

"Careful." Gina held me back by one arm, then peered into the driver's seat. "Good night, you free?" She spoke in an authoritative voice, leaning forward, bending slightly.

"I waitin' for an eleven forty-five."

"Yeah, that's us," I said. "You're Driver—"

"Alright, alright." He exhaled noisily as he leaned over, unlocking the back door nearest to us. "Driver 187."

"We goin' to Club 81."

"I know, I know." He started up. There were no seatbelts in the back. I glanced forward; I could only see part of his face, but his Taxi Driver's ID hung from the rear-view mirror. *Edwin Smith.* "You girls out pretty late."

"Ain' *that* late," Gina said. Her skirt had ridden up, now that she was sitting; she tugged it down again. I was glad I had on pants, although the driver's eyes were firmly on the road.

"Your ma know y'all out this kinda time?"

"Oh, you know her?" Gina tried to make her voice nonchalant.

"Don't have to know her, I know any girl ma. Nobody want their child roamin' bout at midnight."

A police car crossed our path at an intersection ahead. The cab driver slowed slightly, then picked up speed again.

"I got three girls myself. You know where they is?"

"I guess the question is if *you* know where they is," Gina said. I was surprised by the sharpness of her voice. I had never heard her talk that hard to an adult before.

"Alright, alright."

The rest of the drive passed in silence, the night air drifting in through the windows, bringing saltiness with it as we neared the water, and then a thick, rotten smell as we drew closer to the dock. We moved through the eastern end of Shirley Street, passing little side streets. Occasionally, we saw people; two guys going into the gas station store, someone leaning against a broken-down car, a woman and two children walking wearily along the sidewalk.

At Club 81, the driver stopped the meter. "Eighteen fifty."

Gina opened her purse and fished out a twenty. "You could keep the change."

"That's very generous." The driver took the bill. "Now, y'all ga need a pick-up?"

"We could call again—" Gina's voice was sharp. I cut in.

"Yes, please, pick-up at two. It cost anything?"

"No," he told me.

"Alright, thank you."

As we got out, he craned his neck to look back at us. "Hey, girls, lemme give y'all piece a advice. When y'all sneakin' out in the night, don't go walkin' up to no man car and *ask* him if he the driver. Let him tell you his taxi number. That way you don' get swing, ya see?"

"Alright," I said. I supposed he was right, though I hated to admit it.

"Y'all don' carry on too wild inside there."

"Thank you, Daddy," Gina called back.

We edged our way to the door. The bouncer looked us over without interest, waved us in. Gina took my arm and tugged me inside. The room was dark and overwhelmingly purple. The floor was relatively clear. A rap song played. We scurried over to a wall lined with tall red stools.

"You think we should get something to drink?" I said. I had to say it four times, right in Gina's ear, before she heard.

"No, girl, let them buy for *us*." She did not need to say who *them* referred to. We both knew, or at least hoped, that we would each meet someone tonight. Guys whose whispers would make our arms feel like rubber and our legs like molten glass. We would know when we met them. Another song came on, dancehall, and people slowly gathered on the floor, reluctant to appear too eager. Most people there were young, our age, or a little older. Many of the girls wore skirts, like Gina, or jeans tighter than mine, snuggled low on their hips. I leaned back against a stool and tried not to look awkward.

"Look." Gina poked me in the ribs, then peered over at a guy near the speakers on the left. He was tall and he was lean; I couldn't make out much else about him in the dark. He moved his head slightly, and an earring glinted, then disappeared.

"Yeah, he look nice for you," I said, to be encouraging.

"Who you got your eye on?"

No one, was the truth. Something about this place felt familiar in a way I disliked. It was too similar to school, to church socials, places we went with Mummy's sanction. I wasn't sure what to do. What was the point in being here if it wasn't going to be easier than where we always went? Mummy's high heels were beginning to pinch more, as though my feet were continuing to grow, even at this minute. Why hadn't I taken that cotton out before? It seemed out of the question to do anything about it now.

"He would be good for you." Gina looked over at a guy near the bar. We could only see him from the side: baseball cap, jeans that fit, his shirt tucked in, oddly tidy.

"He have a beer belly."

"Well, he might have a nice *personality*," she said, a touch of scorn about her tongue. Yes, this was definitely like the rest of life. I had to be saddled with a nice personality. At least Gina's had a decent build.

"Let's go over," she said. She slipped her bag over her shoulder and tugged me toward the speakers.

"What I gatta come for?"

"Back me up, make sure nobody try snatch me."

We moved through the dancing, which was thick now. The air shook, bass and sweat shuddering. Gina's fingers tightened around my bicep as we moved, bumping people as we went.

"You been drinkin', eh?" I shouted after her, trying to sound sarcastic. She didn't hear. She let go of me as we neared the guy, ran a hand over her hair, and stepped up to him. Was I supposed to stay beside her? Strobed light caught her face, showing a flash of white teeth, then she was thrown back into half-darkness again. The guy nodded slowly, slightly, and spoke. Closer, I could see he was bright-skinned, his hair cut low. He wore a chunky gold ring on his right hand. His eyes moved up and down Gina's form.

"'Scuse me." A male voice behind me. I spun around. "'Scuse me," its owner said again, and moved past, another guy and three girls squeezing by after him.

"Hey, watch it," someone said, this time a woman's voice, on my other side. I turned around to see her drink slosh out of her cup. She sucked her teeth, moving away. Gina was leaning in closer to the guy now, listening, then laughing, tossing her head back. He reached for her hand and she pulled it away, suddenly coy. Then she was wriggling free of her bag, thrusting it into my hands. I felt the heat of her breath, but couldn't hear her words. I didn't need to. I nodded, understood, and pushed my way back to the red stools to sit down.

The music bled into old-school reggae, then vintage dancehall. Gina and the guy were on the dance floor, now visible—her back was to him, he was inches behind her—and now hidden by the crowd. Someone stepped forward to hug a friend and my sister reappeared, wiggling, cutesy-dancing in that tiny dress. She mouthed something to me from the dance floor. I smiled back, but she had already turned away.

I looked back over toward the bar. The guy she had suggested for me was gone. I began to make my way in that direction again, this time easing along the side of the room.

"What you want?" the bartender said, eventually, his face glistening with work.

"Um—a Sprite."

I waited for him to reproach me for not getting something strong, but he took the money, turned away and then back with a cup and my change. I sipped the drink as I edged toward the wall, still clutching Gina's bag. The music had changed again, a newer song I didn't know. The dance floor was packed, Gina nowhere in sight.

"Hey, beautiful."

I turned. The man was short and thin, his red-stained eyes visible even in the dark.

"Hello," I said.

"You ain' dancin' tonight?"

His words were surprisingly clear, despite the music's steady throb. I held my drink up as an answer.

"So finish it. Better yet, put it down, let me buy you another one after we dance."

I looked around for Gina, for help. I spotted her and, miraculously, she looked right at me. She shot me a smile and a thumbs up. I shook my head to signal that I needed her, and the crowd shifted again, a pulsing kaleidoscope. The guy glanced over his shoulder, then back at me.

"I don't take drinks from strangers," I muttered.

"Mark." He held out a hand. The strobes painted his palm yellow, then red. I hesitated, then shook his hand.

"Cold fingers," he said. He leaned in, breath tinged with the yeasty smell of beer. I shifted away. "What's your name?"

A new song came on, and shrieks of approval rose from the crowd. He took hold of my arm as though we knew each other, as though the question had been asked and answered by our shared proximity. I hesitated, but someone squeezed behind me and pushed me forward, agreeing for me. Mark had made a space on the dance floor for us, and tugged me toward him.

Mummy's shoes were leaden, keeping my feet from moving like they should, chaperoning in her absence. It was hotter on the dance floor, like stepping into midday in the twilight of the club. Every time I found the beat, it seemed to change. Mark was behind me. I turned to face him, his eyes were in shadows. I concentrated on the movement of my mother's black pumps, on lifting them, stepping side to side, but they seemed determined to remain as close to the sticky floor as possible. I had seen these shoes on her feet at church, and once for work, when she had to give a presentation. Maybe when she was our age, she'd taken Grammy's shoes and snuck out, though penny loafers and pink house-slippers were all my grandmother ever had in her closet now. The thought of my mother in Grammy's slippers, out on the dance floor, made me smile, despite the dull ache in my belly.

"You look amazing tonight." Mark leaned in close to whisper. His breath was damp and he smelled of too much cologne. The music moved over to a slow song. He put his arms around my waist. I pulled away slightly, but it seemed rude to break totally free. Was there a way to get the handbag between us, somehow? Gina would know what to do. Where was she?

"Hold me, baby." He was close, again, hands cupping my elbows. His voice sickened me—why was he talking as if we were together now? As if he knew something I didn't? The floor was packed; the air felt moist with sweat. "Put your arms around me."

There was a heaviness in his voice, an urgency, as though it was very important, suddenly, that I do what he asked, as though he might become ill if I didn't. I put my arms around his neck. I didn't know why. As the song changed, he pressed himself against the leg of my jeans. I tried to ease away but he held me even tighter. Where was my sister? He let go of me, then slipped behind me, pulling me back onto him. He muttered something—I thought it was "Feel that, baby?" but the noise was jumbling everything. I did feel *that*, if that was what he had said, thick and obvious through three, four folds of fabric. It embarrassed me, and thrilled me, and terrified me. This was what was supposed to happen, this was what we were here for, though Gina and I had not discussed it specifically. And then suddenly, there she was, a glimpse of my sister between bobbing heads and bouncing bodies. The guy she'd been dancing with was wrapped around her, her eyes were closed. It was as though his body was consuming hers; I couldn't make out her arms or midsection, only her face, tilted back toward his. The lights flashed and I saw she was smiling.

"Ease back, baby." Mark was breathless, and this was what I was supposed to do, what everyone was doing, what stolen stilettos promised, what we had tiptoed and planned and broken twelve different rules for. I pushed back against him. Song blended into song. I closed my eyes too. In the dark, it didn't matter how badly I was dancing. It didn't matter that my stomach ached, my head throbbed, that there didn't seem to be space to breathe, that I wanted it to be one fifty-eight, that I was homesick for the rattling window and worn seats of the cab that would be waiting outside. Those dozens, hundreds, of feet stomped and lifted and banged against time until that didn't matter too. I wasn't being squeezed by Mark with no last name, I was being held by the music, by the night.

The first bang was like a popped balloon, the *pap!* muffled by the music's thud. I heard it and tensed. The next followed fast, someone yelled *shot!* and the crowd broke apart like an exploding bomb, even before the third, fourth, fifth were fired. Everyone was running, some toward the main door, some to other exits, some just running wherever their feet dictated. The DJ cut the music, leaving the screams and pants of panic bare. Someone stepped on my foot and I cried out as I elbowed my way toward an Exit sign glowing red. Mark was gone. As I scrambled for the door, I kept looking back for Gina, but it was impossible to see anything. Someone grabbed my arm, shouting something I couldn't hear, then suddenly let go, realizing I wasn't her friend. Then I was outside, the blaring streetlights leaving me squinting. After the press, there was too much space around me. A girl ran by on needle-thin heels, calling for someone named Larry.

"Gina?" I hurried away from the building. People bumped into me as they rushed for their cars. I kept calling out, my voice drowning in a sea of engines starting, doors slamming, noises that belonged to the day. I glimpsed someone who looked like Mark walking past. His eyes met mine a moment. Then he kept going.

"I'm okay, I'm okay." Gina, sweaty and skinny, hobbling on one broken shoe. I threw my arms around her and she pulled me in. "Come, let's go, let's go. It's after two already. You think the cab came?"

Another hard pop cut the air, distant this time. Cold ran over my arms.

"Car backfire," someone shouted with authority. A siren began to whine.

"Look, there," Gina said. At the far end of the parking lot, by a row of old sea grape trees, a cab. "That's our ride."

But as we got closer, I could see it was not a cab at all. The car was empty, and to the side of it, a man was urinating.

The smell rose, sharp and sudden, an insult. Gina let out a small sound like a puppy yipping. The guy turned, called something after us, and Gina's grip on my arm tightened, steering me toward the road.

"He said he would wait." I looked around. The parking lot was almost empty now.

"We could call another one." I passed Gina her bag, and she rummaged inside it for a moment. "My wallet is missing."

My heart dropped almost to my heels. "But I had it on me the whole time."

"It ain' here!" Gina's voice pitched in panic. "We're never gonna get home, we—"

"How long it would take us to walk?"

"Two hours. Longer in heels. And probably get snatch on the way."

"Or we stay here and definitely get snatch."

Gina folded her arms over her chest. I was glad now I had on jeans. The air held a chill.

There was no other way. We began the long walk, huddled, moving as fast as we could. The first few minutes, three cars passed us, probably stragglers from the club. Then the road was empty. I wasn't looking where I was going and got one heel stuck in the slats of a drain. I struggled to loosen my shoe, and its body came away from the heel. I winced as I slipped the other shoe off and carried them both, the whole and the broken, in one hand. Surely our mother had never stolen, then ruined, Grammy's best pair of shoes. Half a minute down the road, something snapped in the brush and I spun around. There was nothing behind us, only a dot of white fluff where we had stopped. I turned away from the disgraced cotton and carried on.

We had been walking for what felt like hours when we passed a man who was going the other way. "Hey, y'all cold tonight?" he called after us.

We shifted closer to each other as we went under a thickness of trees. Someone had hung empty plastic bottles from the branches; they clunked each other clumsily. A horn tooted at us. We spun around, hearts thumping. A truck. It slowed, then stopped just alongside us. "That's the Newburn girls? From across the street?"

"Who's that?" Gina tried to make her voice nonchalant. The truck's window was down, but it was impossible to see the driver.

"This your neighbour," the voice said, and the driver leaned forward. Dino. "What y'all doin' out here? And y'all walkin'?"

"We was out," Gina said, by way of explanation. Her voice sounded empty.

"Along this stretch?" He glanced back. We looked too. Behind us, the roadside had been swallowed up by the night.

Gina shifted. "We had some problems with our ride."

"Hurry up, get in."

We climbed up into the front of the truck, Gina in the middle, then me.

"Y'all lucky I was passing by," Dino said. Gina leaned her head against my shoulder. Her skirt was high; I should have taken the middle, but it was too late now. I arranged the bag over her skin, but Dino's gaze was fixed on the empty road ahead. "Had to drop my girlfriend home, she have work in the morning."

We rode quietly after that, except for the radio. He tuned his radio to a station that played mild music at this time. I had never listened to the radio after 3 a.m. before. It felt different—ethereal somehow.

He pulled into our corner of the street, and backed into his driveway. "I ain' ga make noise outside y'all house. I hope for your sake y'all don' get catch, or Mrs. Newburn ga have y'all heads. And don' tell her I drop you. When she start shellin' out cut hip, I don' wan' her come lookin' for me." He smiled a small, tired grin.

We let ourselves in quietly. In her room, our mother continued to snore. We undressed in the bathroom, turned the tap on just enough to dampen wads of toilet tissue, scrubbed our feet, stuffed our dirty club clothes in a plastic bag, which Gina carried into our room and tucked under her bed. Tamika slept in a tangle of damp sheets. Sometimes we squeezed in together, whispering plans and secrets, but tonight Gina got into her bed and I climbed into mine. Soon, I heard her sounds of rest, the heaviness of her inhale, the slow pace of her breath.

I lay there, listening, unable to fall into dreams. As my

eyes adjusted to the dark, I made out the glinting zipper on Gina's bag, and a long, thin shape protruding from the opening. I slipped out of bed and reached over. My fingers closed over something rubbery, cool. Princess slid out of my sister's bag easily. I crept into bed again, my back to my sleeping sisters. I turned the doll over in my hands. Then, in a twist that caught a beam of light from outside, I saw something on the tip of one foot. A tiny splash of red.

I shoved the doll under the covers and lay still, but my blood rushed, frantic to be free. I felt I would stay awake forever, see dawn pry loose a layer of light and send pink and orange spilling through the windows and over me.

FLOORS

FLOORS ARE FLEXIBLE, CHELSEY REMINDS herself as she squirms on the empty classroom's tiled floor. She wills herself to sink. Two hours have passed since she first prayed for the scuffed squares beneath her chair to open up a channel to the earth's hot wet centre. She has faith.

Somewhere above and behind her, the lab clock clicks seconds by with finality. Each unbending, metallic clink reminds her of the rigidness of words. Of the words. The refusal of *lava* to be spelled with an R. Mister Dick's smirk, which had told her she'd done something wrong. She'd brushed the chalk dust off her hands, hovering between a retreat to her chair and remaining at the front of the class, wondering if she had responded to number five when question eleven had been asked. She'd looked at the board again. What causes a volcano to erupt? *A build-up of gases causes pressure inside the volcano, which then erupts, spewing molten larva.* Someone had snickered.

"Would anyone like to share with Chelsey what is wrong with her answer?"

Larry's arm had shot up. "The volcano spews *lava*."

"Thank you, Larry. Volcanoes are incapable of spewing *larva*, also known," his eyes fell on Chelsey, "as an insect hatchling."

As the class exploded into laughter, Chelsey had returned to her chair and muttered her prayer (in essence, that Mister Dick might be smitten with an incurable virus and Joyce Smith, who had laughed particularly loudly, would meet an early and fiery demise—and that the earth might open its maw through five fathoms of seawater, eleven thousand years of limestone, fifteen metres of topsoil, two feet of concrete foundation, and a quarter inch of vinyl tile, and swallow Chelsey whole). Her wishes were not fulfilled, but Chelsey had returned to the site of her humiliation after school to see if the request might be granted then. The bun at the back of her head made lying flat uncomfortable, but she was certain it would happen soon. Other tiles had parted in the past, like the Red Sea, and there was no reason why this floor shouldn't change its habits too. Why couldn't language be as flexible? Why must the stiffness of that curved lower-case *r* deny the word the meaning everybody knew she had intended?

∞

She knows she dreams by the tremors through her body, particularly at the back of her head, as two women in solid shoes pass by in the hall. There is a layer of haze about her eyelids, and beneath it a field of uncommonly high grass, and in the high grass is Mister Dick. Mister Dick is spreading out a large, foldable world map as if it were a picnic blanket. He is setting down a model of an atom, a desktop-sized plastic skeleton, a globe. Mister Dick is holding up the globe. Inside is some sort of freshly boiled jam. Apricot, perhaps. Is it still bubbling? Silly Mister Dick has put hot jam in the pretty glass globe when the pretty glass globe is cold. The globe shatters, glass and sweetness over grass and skin, all over Mister Dick's grey trousers and white shirt and thick brown plastic glasses. And now, crawling white things. They look like fat, translucent worms. They come and feed on the jam. Mister Dick screams, "The globe is incapable of spewing larva," but neither the larvae nor the globe seem concerned.

Chelsey wakes with a faint smile and discovers the principal standing at her feet.

∞

Chelsey's mother is looking unhappy. "Chelsey," she is saying, "you need to do better in school. First, that mark on your Science test, and now this! I never imagined the principal would call me at my job to tell me one of my children is lying on the floor of the Biology lab fast asleep like some—drunkard! And her skirt not even tucked under her legs to hide her—her underwear!" Mrs. Brown inhales sharply, fortifying herself for the effort of another round of exclamations. "What would your father say? If he were here, what would he say?"

Nothing, Chelsey wants to reply, as she looks down at the dining table, but this is not the time or place for such remarks. She shifts in her chair, tucks the pleated skirt under her legs. Her father, were he able to say anything, would say what he said last. Floors are flexible. And earth moves.

∞

That night, Mrs. Brown asks, "And when are you getting started on this project that Mr.—"

"—Dick?"

"Mr. *Richard* assigned your class?"

Chelsey would like to designate *never* as her intended start date, but settles for saying nothing instead.

"Fine." Mrs. Brown sets the stack of plates on the counter so firmly they should break. "You can start tonight."

∞

Chelsey sits at the table after dinner to begin.

"What are you working on?" her brother asks.

"Science project."

"With that in your hand?"

Chelsey sets the programme down to one side. Her father and his vital numbers, 1974–2019, stare up at her, a wry smile in his eyes. *Service Of Thanksgiving For The Life Of.*

"What's the project on?"

"I dunno. Some dumb science thing."

"You better not let Mummy hear you talking sloppy like that."

"Like what?"

"Saying *dunno*. It's slang."

"Piss off." Chelsey grabs up the programme. Her feet take her to the kitchen, then through the back door and into the panting night. It is heavy with fallen guavas, nibbled at by rats and lizards, now fermenting to soily fruit brandy. The spheres yield as she stumbles through them, pink seeds clinging to her bare soles. She comes to the jars; rows and rows, sprigs of lime leaves in each, air holes cut in the tops. *Watch them close*, her father had said. *If you don't let them loose as soon as they hatch, their wings go to waste and they die.*

∞

"Did you do that project?" says Lorraine to No One In Particular. The classroom is full of cardboard creations, galactic models (*not actual size*, declares a disclaimer taped to the side of Gina's Milky Way), toothpick buildings and macaroni condos.

"Hey, Chelsey, nice volcano. Got any larrrrr-va in there?"

The buzz and chatter is loud enough that no one else hears Joyce's comment or her elongated, trilled *r*. Chelsey stands protectively in front of her paper re-creation, an inverted cone made of taped-together fuchsia construction paper. She has bent it in places to accommodate the stacked jars underneath. She is tempted to peep at the jars again, but Mister Dick enters the room, so she sits.

"Good morning, students. I see there is quite a lot of activity this morning. I'll walk about and see a bit of what you've got here."

Mister Dick explores Maria's cardboard piece showing the earth's layers and Trevor's depiction of Saturn's rings, fashioned from cotton wool and coat hangers, before coming to Chelsey's volcano. He walks around the structure. "Marks off for pink—mountains are not pink." He peers through the hole at the top, down into the maze of dangerously stacked jars. "Come here, everyone." The class crowds around to see. "Chelsey has done something almost clever—she has filled her volcano with jars of what are supposed to be larvae—presumably to represent lava. Unfortunately," here he pauses, reaches into the bowels of Chelsey's creation, his hand just fitting through the space at the top, twists once, twice, and comes up with a lid, "the larvae are still entrapped in cocoons, and incapable of erupting from the volcano.

It looks like Chelsey's project is still dormant." Someone snickers. The children redisperse. Mister Dick moves on to Lorraine's project, a series of paper planes suspended from skewers in front of a battery-operated fan.

Chelsey's eyes are closed in prayer. Feet crave the parting of tiles, topsoil, limestone and sea. She knows the floor can move. She sees her father, laying the last kitchen tile, pressing grout between the crevices. Saying "don't walk here yet, these aren't set." Feels the ripe guavas in her hands, warm off the tree and sap still flowing fresh. Feels the brush of something, soft as dust, on her wrist. Something, something tiny and white. Screams "worm!" and drops the green and yellow fruits, sends them scattering. Daddy reaching to pick them up and slipping, squashed guavas and loose tiles, his head against the floor. Cemetery soil a week later, sliding almost back into place, a small mound of dirt the only evidence of the displacement. Of course the floor is flexible. But not *cemetery*—all those syllables and not one place for facts to shift.

Chelsey's eyes open to Mister Dick's back. Lightly perched on the top of his head, a hatchling preens, balanced on six spindly legs.

She rips off the pink cone. Opens one jar, and another, and another. At first, nothing.

Then a burst of black and sapphire swirls up, a choke of flutter, a dervish of fragile, multi-hued things. The floor begins to whirl, Mister Dick obscured by dozens of damp wings.

YOU CAN ALWAYS COME HOME

BREAD

WHEN IT HAPPENED, MY MOTHER would scuttle into
the kitchen and begin baking bread. The bread rose from
a low, silent lump into a lighthearted dough that could not
be discouraged, that expanded, puffed up, spread its aroma
out into our home and beyond, under the door and through
the corridors of the fifth floor, blessing the air with cinnamon and the low, almost-human scent of yeast.

My father would reach for the remote with an impa-
tient sigh and turn up the TV. "Some people," he would
say, "insist on living like trash. Can't bring them up from
the gutter." Below the television's numbing blare, I could
feel, if not entirely hear, the raised voices from next door,
the sudden thumps, the odd, bird-like shrieks.

But my mother would gather herself up, quietly lifting

her stand mixer onto the counter, heaving a ten-pound bag of flour up beside it. She always used organic whole wheat, sold in brown paper packages from a small grocery store that had clean wood floors and a perpetual aroma of fish.

"I don't know," my father grumbled, "why you waste your money. Between hard drugs and pesticides, which one you think is going to kill these bums first?"

My mother said nothing, only tore the bag open with a decisive-sounding rip, then set aside yeast and warm water till the mixture frothed, thrilled by the pinch of sugar she added in. She said little while she measured and stirred and kneaded. Her bread would rise, then bake, then rest on the cooling racks, plump and warm, like a secret freshly told. In the morning, she would pack it up, and the two of us would take a load down to the soup kitchen. It was a miracle, every time.

"Like we're living in the ghetto," he continued, settling deeper into his easy chair. I had never lived in a ghetto, and as far as I knew, neither had he. How would he know what it was like? Had the low, long bungalow we'd given up in Nassau, on a quiet street shaded over with dilly trees and sea grapes, become some sort of exotic slum now that we lived far away?

∞

Our condo was small and tidy, magically suspended five storeys in the air, with another twelve floors stretching above us into the sky. The corridor's flooring had been recently replaced. Light bulbs in the hallway never seemed to go out. The parking area did not reek of urine, it had no smell at all, in fact, and felt dark, chilled, empty, even when the lot was full, even when daylight crept in as far as it could down the ramp. Our building was guarded by gates and digitally-locked doors, but when I parted the blinds in our unit and peered down, I could see strangely dressed figures, their bodies thick with grimy clothes, as though they wore their whole wardrobes at once. They moved, some with ferocious focus, barrelling down the sidewalk toward a place beyond our view. Others bunched together like ants around a dropped mint, gathering nourishment from some invisible thing at their core. Even through the thick, double-glazed windows, I could hear the quick clink of empty bottles bouncing along in shopping carts.

"Is this the same cart the people below use?" I asked my mother once at the supermarket, as we gathered up bunches of green-tipped bananas and packages of black-berry yogurt.

"Yeah, Sherlock, it's Pinky's favourite one. Look, see the marks on the handle? That's where he likes to chew when he gets hungry. See that dent? He hit his head there."

My mother hushed my brother, but it was weeks before I would touch a cart again.

∞

Pinky had long, greasy hair, which he kept pulled back into a ponytail that protruded from a baseball cap of unspecified colour. He wore an odd collection of clothing: a t-shirt with a jacket, long pants and some sort of tunic over top. He was almost certainly not Black, because his hair was very straight, but other than that, he could have been almost any sort of person, with any sort of real name in any of the strange languages people here spoke. My brother had nicknamed him "Pinky" because of the teddy bear he kept in the front of his cart. It was the colour of bubblegum-flavoured toothpaste. Unlike the toothpaste, the bear did not sparkle, or if it did, the shimmers were not visible from our height.

Pinky's cart was perpetually rattling, a heavy, multi-layered shake. I found it strange that my brother could so keenly pick out Pinky's teeth marks on the handle of the supermarket cart when he did not seem to understand what was going on when the television volume went up and our mother's baking began.

∞

She hummed as she gathered her ingredients. Water was warming on the stovetop; yeast sat waiting, patient; sugar, cinnamon, nutmeg, all lined up beside a cardboard carton of eggs and a container of whole milk.

"More nutrition," she told me, or the dough, it was

difficult to know which of us she addressed. "The people need a little extra calcium, you know."

The deft crack of an egg on the side of the bowl, then another, the slick innards trying to sidestep the mixer's hook before they were caught, split, absorbed. The mixer's whir was steady and high. Still, next door, I could hear voices filtering through the thin walls, occasionally a crash, a heavy thud. My mother switched the machine off, lifting the dough onto the flour-dusted counter and pulling it, turning it, pushing it, slapping it, then folding it and beginning again.

∞

In the morning, my mother slipped into the room my brother and I shared, tiptoeing past his bed, moving quietly so as not to disturb his steady snores. She touched my shoulder, my knee, her palm heating my skin through the sheets. I was awake already, expecting her, but pretended to be surprised. The condo was quiet, still. The bread, lined up on a grid of cooling racks covering the table, stood ready. We slid each loaf into its own clear plastic bag.

"Make sure to squeeze all the air out, that keeps them fresh longer," she said. Her long, tapered fingers moved quickly as they knotted each bag. She loaded the bags into a box, then sent me off to freshen up. I only addressed the most basic requirements; I revelled in the secret warmth of my body, still undisturbed from sleep.

My face washed, my mouth sweet from pink toothpaste, we stepped out into the hall. "Hold on, there." My mother reached for my head and tugged off the purple satin scarf I wore to bed. She folded it up and draped it over our door-knob. We both glanced at our neighbours' door. Their condo was strangely quiet, as though righting itself back to balance. My mother shook her head, then together we lifted the box of bread and moved toward the elevator.

∞

That night, the thumping and yelling swelled again. As usual, my father turned up the sound on the television. My brother seemed to register nothing.

"I'm not drunk! I'm not fucking drunk!" The words were clearer than before. Perhaps our open windows made them so. Perhaps the voice was louder. My father increased the television's volume again. An ad for soda came on, blaring joyously.

"The taste of the tropics," the television exclaimed, "in every bottle!" Steel pan music played as a conga line of animated fruit pranced across the screen.

My brother heaved himself up off the sofa as though his long, thin frame was inconvenient to move. "I'm out," he said, swiping his skateboard.

My father glanced away from the screen. "Where you think you're going?"

"I can't think straight in here."

My mother looked up from her recipe book. "It's pretty late."

"Relax, man."

My father's gaze fixed on my brother. I wondered if there would be a standoff, my brother planting himself, stubborn, in front of the doorway, my father hoisting him up by his collar, my mother draping observations between them like cobwebs. My father pressed a button on the remote; the TV fell silent, pictures still dancing across the screen. He rose from his seat, his head tilted slightly as though he was tuning in, listening hard to catch a whisper. He seemed both relaxed and ready to spring. "What's that, now?"

Next door, there was a smothered yelp, sharp and high, like a dog's paw had been stepped on, hard. My brother stood, defiant, a moment, then dropped his skateboard. It fell with a rough clatter that coincided with a thud from the other side of the wall. My father's head straightened; he sank back into his seat, unmuted the TV.

"Depression hurts," the television advised us.

My brother disappeared into our room. I followed behind him. The lights were off. He lay on his bed, face to the ceiling, legs bent. He seemed too long for his single bed. He might have told me to get out, but tonight, he said nothing. I kneeled on the floor in the small space between my bed and the bureau, facing the window to see if I could spot Pinky. The street below us whirred with activity. A bundle of untidy-looking people clustered under a tree. In the grassy square further down the road, tiny forms came and went. I imagined my brother, reduced to the size of a gnat, weaving between the strange figures. It made me feel faintly ill.

"You see Pinky?" I asked. It was more of a conversation-opener, since my brother was on his side facing the wall.

"You can't find nothing else to do?"

"No," I answered.

I turned back to the window. There were plenty of people with shopping carts, but none with a pink teddy in the child seat. My brother was listening to music now, earphones snaking from his phone to either side of his head. The tinny beat made me feel more alone; I knew the song was happening, but couldn't hear it, not really.

Resigned, I went back into the living room. My father's head had dipped in sleep, the television still shouting out news headlines. In the kitchen, my mother's back was turned. She was bent over her quickbreads cookbook, scrutinizing the pages, studious, earnest. I reached for the key and swipe card that lived on the counter, slipped them into my pocket, and let myself out.

As I stepped out into the corridor, my heart pounded. The familiar hallway, cool air piping out from the ceiling, seemed a faintly frightening place on my own. I leaned against the sturdiness of our door for a moment, then tip-toed down the hall. I held my breath as I passed the unit beside ours, not wanting to hear anything terrible, half hoping I would.

The stairwell's bare concrete amplified the click of the door shutting behind me. The fluorescent bulbs emitted a shrill, constant whine, as though glowing mosquitoes lit the place. Through the strip of window that ran straight down to the ground floor, I could see the steady glow of streetlights, traffic's shifting glint. I made my way down almost to the bottom floor, then pressed my face against a window. The people below were close enough to hear, nearly close enough to touch. Just across the street, a man stumbled into the back of a parked car. He swore at the car, his voice hard and rough, as though his throat was lined with sandpaper and small stones. A pair of women walked by in miniskirts. One had short, light-coloured hair; the other's was long and dark. The dark-haired one seemed to glance over at me, and I crouched down. I saw her raise an arm, wave, and shout something. Her friend laughed, a free, tearing sound, and pulled her away down the sidewalk.

Then I saw Pinky, his cart rattling as he neared me. He was shorter than I had thought. He wore his cap jammed over his head, almost the same way my brother did. His hat was dark grey, maybe not originally that colour, and seemed part of his head. I couldn't see his face. His cart was full of glass bottles that bumped together cheerfully. The pink bear bounced slightly. Further down the street, two men were talking, gesturing wildly. I saw one give the other a push, then take a shove himself. The first man pulled his arm back, then sent it sideways into the other man's jaw. The punched man fell back onto the sidewalk. He struggled to get up, and was pushed down. Raised an arm, and was pushed down again. I turned and ran up the stairs, my body moving faster than my feet, tripping over myself. I caught my balance and turned back to the window. The man was still down, the other hunched over him, drawing a fist back. The man on the ground was shouting for help, I was sure of it, but as I moved further up, I heard nothing.

∞

I unlocked our door, wondering if I was returning to punishment or eager embraces. I let myself in, slipped down the hallway. In the living room, the television still blared. My father's chin rested on his chest, his eyes closed. My mother looked up at me as I crossed the room.

"You alright, sweetie?" she asked.

In the kitchen, the dough had already risen. I wondered how long I'd been gone. I seemed to remind my mother of something; she set her book down, stood up, turned the television off, and peered into the oven, cracking the door open a little bit.

"Extra big batch tonight," she said sadly. And then, "The kitchen says donations have been down this year."

That night, instead of leaving all the bread to cool, she wrapped one loaf in paper towels, then dropped it into a paper bag so it wouldn't sweat and spoil. She saw me watching and brought a finger to her lips. She unlocked our front door, and I followed her, saw her pad to our neighbours' door, rest the bag down, knock, then scamper back. Her step was light, almost playful.

"Sometimes goodness can't wait till morning," she said.

In the kitchen, she hummed as she spread clean dish-cloths over the remaining loaves. "Time for bed, pumpkin," she told me, and I went.

I lay there for a while, listening to the sound of water moving through pipes, the soft opening and closing of drawers in my parents' bedroom, the light switch being flicked off. I got out of bed and slipped into the living room. I sat next to the silenced television, just behind the dining table, smelling the cooling bread. This time she had put herbs and whole garlic cloves into the dough. I pressed my back against the adjoining wall. I could hear the woman's voice, low, and the man's, rumbling, but the wall between us swallowed up their words.

∞

My mother and I woke early the next morning. Opening the door, her arms full of bread, she gasped and nearly dropped the box of loaves. On our *Welcome* doormat lay last night's gift. It had been savagely torn open, ripped into chunks and dumped back into its bag. She snatched it up. We bustled into the elevator, my mother's face unreadable. In the parking garage, she opened the door to the room that held three dumpsters, and hurled the spoiled bread into the mouth of the nearest one.

∞

"Did you hear," my father asked over dinner, "about what happened last night?"

"Timothy?" My mother's fork hovered over her plate, holding a scoop of peas and rice precariously. "Later."

My father shook his head in disgust. "Across the street from us. Couple jonesers got in a fight. They say the one almost killed the other."

"Outside our building?" My brother leaned forward, eager for gore.

"Pretty much. To think we came here to get away from this. The one man, whole left side of his face was split open—"

"No." My mother's voice cut through, sharp. There was a silence for two, three seconds. She cleared her throat, and when she spoke again, her voice had softened. "Not at the table."

"Was it Pinky?" My brother was undeterred.

"I don't know who these people are." My father attacked his piece of chicken with his fork. "Far as I'm concerned, no one would miss one or two less of them anyway."

"No, baby, it wasn't Pinky." My mother's voice was smooth again. She reached over, gave my arm a quick squeeze. "Pinky's just fine."

Later, I slipped out of bed and padded into the living room. I could hear my parents' muffled voices from their bedroom. I peered out of the window. Below, a few thin wreaths had been laid out on the sidewalk. I let the curtain drop. Next door was silent. I wondered if our neighbours were out, or if their voices were just hushed tonight, like ours.

∞

The next night, the power went out. The electricity vanished with a sudden tug, the television image closing up on itself, sound pulled in. From the sofa, my brother glanced up briefly from his phone and sucked his teeth. My father swore.

"Ha ha, Daddy cussed," my brother crowed, as if the dark would shield him from discipline.

All the buildings around ours had lost power too, giving us a rare, thick, city dark. My mother began to rummage for candles and flashlights, slowly illuminating the place. My father still clutched the now-defunct remote and my brother lay sprawled on his back on the sofa, while my mother distributed brightness, her face lit up like a saint's.

"Well, I'm gonna go to the skateboard park," my brother said.

"You aren't going anywhere." My mother set down the last candle, a large flower half-melted into an awkward pink clump, with a bang.

Then it started. Without the television blaring, without the gentle rumble and buzz of the modem and router, the fridge and freezer, clocks and phone chargers and fluorescent bulbs with their faint falsettos, without the distraction of the mixer's late-night whir, the sounds from next door were as clear as if they were coming from inside our home. He was calling her names. Some I knew, but others were foreign to me, the familiar and the new pressed together. We could hear her screaming insults back at him. She was so real, more real, even, than Pinky. The remote slipped from my father's fingers and clunked onto the floor.

"I'm going over there." My mother spoke so quietly I thought only I might have heard her. She strode to the door—I slunked over beside her, clinging close.

"Margaret, don't get involved," my father said. "These people aren't our business."

There was a crash, the sound of many things breaking, and the woman's voice, raw. She was begging.

"He'll kill her."

I expected her to tell me to stay inside, but she didn't stop me when I scampered after her. We stepped into the hallway and the door shut behind us. The corridor was lit with white emergency bulbs that cast strange shadows, making my mother seem mysterious and long. We could hear even more clearly now: the woman wailing, *thump*, some item shattering, *thump*. My mother crossed the distance between our doors in three broad strides. She pounded on the door with her fist.

"Open up!" she commanded. My father called to us from our own doorway, trying to lure us back. "Open this door! You stop this! You leave her alone!" She rattled their doorknob. "Open up!" Her banging reverberated, and inside, beyond the door, silence.

The hallway lights flashed back on. The low, choral hum of appliances returned, breaking the spell. Her fist dropped to her side, fingers still balled together in a knot. My father put an arm around her shoulders, guiding her back to our own door. There was nothing to do but follow.

"Mum?" My brother was still on the sofa, his face oddly lit, the lamplight and candles competing with his phone's glow. "That was you?" His thick eyebrows were raised, his eyes wide in his acne-spotted face.

My father held her. She was stiff, still, with rage. Finally, he let her go. "Get your mother some water," he told me.

In the kitchen, I filled a glass. I pressed my ear to the shared wall. Nothing.

My father slumped into his chair. "Sit down, Marg." He reached for the remote.

"You turn that TV on, I'll cut your fucking hand off!" My mother spat the words out like bullets, then clapped a hand over her mouth, too late.

My father rose, frowning, staring at her as though he had not been prepared for this possibility. He opened his mouth, then shut it again. He set the remote down on the chair, moved quickly toward the bedroom, closed the door behind him. Mummy stayed, hand pressed over her lips. Through the silence, there was nothing from next door.

∞

I heard her moving around in the middle of the night. The scent of yeast pulled me out of bed. From the hallway, I could hear the whir of the mixer, the quick metal swish of knife against measuring cup, levelling off flour.

She moved swiftly, precisely. Dough rested already, covered with warm, damp cloths. The table was filled with loaves. How long had she been going? Couldn't have been enough rising time, the bread should have been emerging from the oven heavy and dumb. Instead, the domes were perfect: curved, round, browned lightly, flecked with dried fruit. Sweet spices—cinnamon, nutmeg, pimento, mace—hung thick in the air. She was candying nuts for her maple pecan loaf. I sat and watched her toast the wrinkled brown halves in the pan, then toss in a slab of butter, spoonfuls of sugar that relented to the heat and became molten and dangerous. As the first light began to strike the condo's glass, she clicked the oven off and set down the last loaves to cool. Bread flooded the table, crowded the counters. She had placed extras on the dining chairs, more on clean sheets on the floor.

She put on her shoes, then began to ferry the loaves over to the people beside us. She stacked an enormous mound in front of their unit on our yellow picnic blanket, so that when they opened their door, pillowy loaves—raisin, garlic herb swirled with grated cheddar, walnut sourdoughs, whole wheat freckled with flax—would tumble in.

When she was done, we sat together on the living room floor and waited. My father avoided looking at us and quietly left for work. My brother emerged, took in the disarray of the kitchen, then slipped away. When I heard the door to our neighbours' place click open, my mother didn't speak, didn't move. Then there were heavy footsteps retreating, then nothing.

She stood up, after a time. "Maybe she's found it. Maybe she's out there now." She opened our door. I followed, trying to make no sound.

The bread tower had, predictably, fallen over. The neighbours' door was wedged open by loaves. More bread tumbled in through their doorway. My mother took a step forward, peered into their home. Her breath caught.

The woman was tall and thick. Even bent down, she looked to be my father's height, at least. She wore a pink nightie, and a purple scarf on her head like mine. A long braid escaped from under the satiny cloth and snaked down her back. She was on her hands and knees on the hardwood floor of her kitchen, its layout a mirror of ours. She was sopping up broken glass and a clear liquid, and spatters of red, with a sponge, big and brown. A slash was open on one of her arms.

I touched my mother's arm—she was still, except for her eyes. They darted around, taking in the woman, the carnage. Suddenly, she looked down at me. Her arm shot out toward my head and before she could touch me a sound escaped my mouth, an ugly squeak; I didn't recognize it. But I felt no pain, only a bareness, a waft of cool. I lifted my hand to my head and felt the tight crinkle of my hair. My mother stuffed my scarf into her pocket. A purple tail hung loose, refusing to hide.

The woman looked up at us and froze. Her eyes were guilty, as though she had been caught doing something shameful. It was only then I realized she wasn't using a sponge. She straightened up, the loaf hanging loose in her hand. It was a raisin one swirled through with sweet, broken glass embedded in the softness, the insides stained watery red.

My mother sprang to life again. She began grabbing up the hunks of bread that wedged the door open. It banged closed on the woman, the mess, the stained loaf, her split arm, the scarf. My mother hurried to gather the remaining loaves into our condo, shovelling me in with them.

And now, on the balcony, she is releasing the rescued loaves, letting them drop from five storeys high. As she rushes back in for more, the people below are gathering, arms raised. There is Pinky, his shopping cart abandoned, the pink teddy bear lolling in the child's seat. Pinky strains to look up, like all the others, scampering, leaping to gather a loaf. My mother drops the last one, then disappears inside, races past me into the kitchen. The crowd begins to disperse when it becomes clear the shower of bounty has run dry. Pinky remains, staring up, his cap shading his eyes.

Then my mother returns, hugging the entire mixer to her chest. The base bumps against her hip, the bowl still sticky. The dough hook beckons, a metallic comma. She heaves the mixer onto the balcony's edge. It balances for a moment, the metal bowl catching light like a mirror, blinding me. Below us, Pinky cranes his neck, face upturned, waiting.

NIGHT FAIR

ON THE PLANE BACK HOME I'M next to Blabbermouth Bill who can't take a signal when I shove a mint in my mouth, turn toward the window, close my eyes. *Where are you from, are you in school in Atlanta, I hear Bahamians are real friendly, is that right? And they like to dance, right? Caribbean people really love to dance. I knew a girl from Jamaica, if you put on music you couldn't keep her still for nothing.* To shut him up I tell him about Night Fair. *There's music and dancing. You should go, you'd like it,* I say, then run my hands over my new low haircut, put earphones on, turn up the music loud, sit very still.

∞

Of course we gone dance, Sister says on my second night back as she dabs concealer on her neck. She turns up the stereo, one of Grampy's songs recorded the year Daddy was born. Crackly voice, rude brass, twangy banjoes. *I don't know why you so uptight. Come on. Your own granddaddy used to dance all the time. Plus, everyone is dance at Night Fair.*

I think of Grampy, old man mimicking boyhood, shilling-pence shows, proud that tourists thanked his two-step in the sandy sun with candy and small change. Didn't that humiliate him? I want to ask, but the music is too loud, and anyway, Sister's busy mimicking Grammy's one-one clip dicey-doe. *Fine, whatever*, I say, *I'll go.*

She dabs powder over her face and shoulders, readjusts her orange tube top. *Well at least you ain't lose all your sense when you let them shave your head.*

∞

The streets downtown are full. Nearly-naked girls walk, thin fabric curling their nipples, hips, winking like *joke's on us.* Their sharp shoes call *fallmedown*, high-perched feet clacking past sun-faced men beerbottle high. Streetlights piss a pale yellow glow. Sweetsmoke boys lure from shadows *kss kss kss, slim, hey hey lookhere slim whathappen girl you stuckup, eh?*

I don't know why you dragging me to this, I tell Sister again, trying to look busy as we pass the boys by, their glazed eyes poinciana-red. They aren't looking at us much anyway. In front of us, three girls who talk quick and four-teen. A boy's hand lashes out and curls around a wrist, fast fingers calling her in. The caught girl giggles, eyes flash, hard brown pearls.

Night Fair changed since last summer, I say. *I swear there used to be less smoke, more clothes.*

Why clothes such a good thing? Sister grabs my arm, *See Shenique and Tamara*, pulls me through the crowd. I'm not sure where she's taking me until we're right in front of them. They look almost unchanged. Shenique's hair highlighted honeygold, black pants snug. She hugs me, purple gauze bell sleeves fluttering. *Gii–iii–iiiirrl, lookatyou look how you change so much*, runs a hand over my head. *How come you cut it?* I hug Tamara on her left side, since on the right she has sprouted a growth. *Yours?* I ask. She nods, bored.

We goin' dancing, Sister says. *You know you can't carry no baby in the dance.*

Let me see if I could find Mummy so she could keep her, Tamara says. *You want hold Babygirl? I tired.* Tamara leans the growth toward me and I relieve her of the warm brown bundle.

Hello, I say. *Hey, little girl. What your mummy been doing since I was away, hey? What your mummy been doing so? Hey? She been gettin' in trouble? Hey, baby?* I try to adjust her to sit comfortably but it's not like a little handbag over the shoulder. How you supposed to hold these things,

I wonder. I test her out balanced on my hip like Tamara did. Her small fat hands cling to my skyblue shirt tight. Where do they learn to hold on so?

Shenique falls in step next to me, as next as possible while we squeeze through the crowds. There's music now, it makes it hard to talk. *How you like Atlanta? Girl, I can't believe you cut your hair. All that long pretty hair.* I laugh. The music takes it up. Shenique notes its fastfast beat, her fingers clip, snap-shoes clicking somewhere beneath all the loud.

See them there, Tamara mouths, pointing out a food stall. We shortcut between tents, the vendors black-glaring as we squeeze between tables of sternos and steamy food pans in our rickety stilettoes. There's her mother and sister eating conch fritters wrapped in brown paper stained clear with grease. The sister is shorter, less showing, with less to show, but her jeans whisper *don't like you* to her navel and slip low. The mother hugs me. *Girl look at you, change so much, you's woman now.* I lean the baby toward her. Babygirl whimpers, so I point her at Tamara instead. Little fingers claw my arm. *Give her to her grammy so we could go,* Tamara says. The mother cuts her eye at Tamara. *What you want leave baby with me for? Where y'all going so, why you can't take her? Alright fine fine, pass her, fine.* Her hot hands pry the small fingers loose. Babygirl stiffens, flings her head.

Her cries fade away as we near the dance area. The music draws frantic, and there's a long line to get in. In front of us are two of the girls from before, laughing at the ticket guy, tugging at their feathery shirts. The music shakes through our legs as the line moves slow, each step bringing us closer to the bigspeaker shrine. Junkanoo music, Sister, Shenique already moving, torsos tilting to melody, clench, tilt again. Tamara and I edge forward. She seems as out of place as I feel. I don't remember her liking dancing that much. *You don't mind leaving her?* I yell over the music. She shrugs. *Sometimes I need a break.* I wonder, How you get this baby anyway, you say you wasn't having any kids, and we edge forward and music pounds and we pay and squeeze on inside.

There is no dance floor. Rocky ground, makeshift fence, sheet-plastic walls. No chairs—you ain' business sitting down—*how y'all enjoying yourself* DJ blares crowd screams bumps and throbs, thin arms wave, backsides, thighs, shakeshake frantic on beat. I glance down at my blouse, still mashed from Babygirl's fists. Tamara shuffles in a distracted side-to-side. *Mummy used to tell me I was gone spoil her always holding her, now she so spoil she don't even want me leave.* I nod. Something over the music's thud and pulse like Babygirl crying but couldn't be and Sister drags me, one hand, Tamara in the other, to the centre of centre. Music scratchy shift: soca dub and base up, *thumthum* beat hungry, earthy, blood pulse-y, hone-y, heady, steady *thumthum* feed, bathe baby, schoolfee pay, lightbill, cable, grocery, *thumthum* ground cover in grapes, yesterday's dinner pay

for with wine *thumthum* mash feet move them move them
or starve *thumthumthumthum thumthum*. My eyes close
and I make myself listen dancegirl dance.

Fingers on my shoulder bring me back. My eyes open.
A small white spotlight cuts through din and press and stops
on Sister, face a damp brown moon. It's a video camera;
holding it is Blabbermouth Bill and he turns, points the
spotlight on Tamara's circling hips then on the two teenage
girls. Their sassy bits bounce. Sees me, pants out *smallworld
I remember you natives friendly music party dance wanna
honey camera dance.* Baby howl white hot light girlbits
bounce pulse pump Grampy two-step tight Tamara Sister
my fingers fumble a shoe loose arm pull back

aim tight

set fly glass smash

white light scatter everywhere

stop.

One hand up—smoke frozen, shirts midflutter, music
stuck, air thick, one low bass beat hang neat half open
thum. Pull myself up, grab hold of that hard dark bulk,
pull, hip-cradle it, my own broke Babygirl.

Bare feet fly me over, broke glass camera piece between
heels bodies twist I push run between them one two
onetwo onetwoonetwo two twostep away, fast, girl, *dance
girl dance girl*

dance dance girl

dancedance.

SWITCHER

PASTOR'S WIFE CAME EACH MORNING at eleven. "God ain' lead Kevvie back to us today," she would say, as though the house, a low one-storey set back from the road, painted cream with green trim and green front and back doors, was a church he had strayed from. Then she would offer to pray. After the first week, Annette wanted to say "No, thank you," and, after the second week, just "No." In the third week, she found herself wanting to take Pastor's wife by her tightly slicked ponytail and bang her shiny, high forehead into the coffee table again and again.

"Sure," Annette would say, instead.

"Let's kneel." And Pastor's wife would sink down onto the large white tiles, hands outstretched and head lowered. Annette sat but kept her head bowed while Pastor's wife spoke in rising, fervent tones. "Lord Jesus, we come to you in prayer regarding little Kevvie Rahming. Lord Jesus, you know where Kevvie is, you alone have the power to lead him back to us."

As the prayer proceeded, Annette would keep her eyes closed. She detached her self from her body, a gentle unhooking. She rose and rose, viewing her body from above, head bowed, hands upturned, palms to the ceiling.

Pastor's wife's voice would rise, too, almost shouting. "And just protect him, Lord, wherever he is, he just a child, Lord"—her voice always broke with *child*—"and Lord, we know the children are precious to you, we are all precious, Lord Jesus, all precious in your sight . . ."

Annette would rise and rise. But at the ceiling, she felt herself trapped, unable to move beyond the boundaries of the room.

"In the sweet name of Jesus, we pray, God Almighty. Amen."

"Amen," Annette would hear herself say. "Amen."

∞

After the prayer, Pastor's wife would have a glass of switcher. Annette always had water instead; she found the switcher too strong, but Kevvie liked it that way, sickly sweet, and so tart it made you wince. After Pastor's wife had gone, leaving behind a purple lipstick-print on the glass and the pious scent of Irish Spring, Annette would go into the kitchen, pour out a cup of the drink, and drop a few ice cubes into it. She would set the switcher out on the back doorstep. The cubes would crack in protest, jostling each other before they rose to rest and, slowly, quietly, disappeared.

∞

In the evening, Annette's sister would come.

"Nettie!" Tracy would holler, before the car engine was turned off.

"The mouth reach," Annette's husband would mutter, getting up from the sofa to open the door. "Tracy, how you doin'?"

From the kitchen, Annette would hear her sister pulling at breath, winded by the exhausting trek from car to front door. "Lord. These steps ga kill me dead." Then would she lower her voice to an indiscreet whisper and ask, "Any news?"

"No, Tracy. Nothing yet."

Tracy would update her on the people she had spoken to about Kevin. "I gone by the station, tell them my little nephew been missin' *twenty-eight days* and police ain' find nothin' yet." "Patrick and the boys gone out after dinner to look around out Carmichael, you know plenty bush round there . . ." "My whole book club put up posters in their neighbourhoods. Time to bring this baby home."

Sometimes, Annette would hear Dennis begin to cry. He was a big man, not fat, but strong across his shoulders, rum barrel–thick in the waist, with deeply bowed legs. She would recognize the sound—*a-hee-hee-hee*—between Tracy's protests.

"Oh, Lord, I ain' mean to upset you, Dennis."

A-hee-hee-hee.

"We all here to help, we ga find him."

Annette would remove herself to the backyard, stepping past the glass of switcher on the step. There, the sky ballooned out, billowy black, high enough to let her breathe. Annette would lean against the dilly tree. Higher up, she could see half-formed fruit, skins rough and brown. She could hear voices inside, but the words were soft and indistinct.

∞

In the night, she lay in bed, knowing where he was. Beside Lake Cunningham. In the mangroves way out Adelaide. In a twine of bush in Yamacraw. Under one of the silk cotton trees behind the main post office. At the top of the bridge. At the bottom of the sea.

∞

When the police car pulled up outside the house, Dennis was watching the news. In the kitchen, Annette sliced through the heart of a sour. She came to the front door, the smell of citrus tart on her hands. The young officer had taken off his hat. His hair was cut low, as though he were going back to school.

As the officer spoke, Annette closed her eyes. Outside on the back step, a small settling noise, ice moving in drink. Annette moved quickly away from the officer, through the dining room, into the kitchen, toward the back door, her heart rising. She knew what she would find. The cup up off the step, Kevvie's two hands around it, ice clinking dully. His eyes peering at her over the top of the cup as he gulped the switcher down, a little spilling, tart and sweet. Round face, bare feet, smooth little-boy skin. Fumbling with the lock, Annette felt her eyes begin to sting. She swung the door open.

"Kevvie?"

On the back step, the plastic cup sat alone. Its ice had settled, the switcher closer to the rim.

"Kevvie?" she said again, evening swallowing her words. "Kevvie? That's you?"

FRESH MILK

ALL DAY, CLOUDS HAVE HUNG AROUND like boys on a street corner, shifting, waiting. We reach the new building just after three, but the sky feels like dusk. The driver leaves the cab running as he gets out, opens the trunk, sets the boxes and bags and suitcases on the scrappy grass, then steps back, hands in his pockets. While Mummy pays, Paul balanced on one hip, I turn toward the apartments. I imagined living on the second floor would be special, sitting high above the roofs of others, overlooking a beautiful view. Instead, we face an empty plaza slowly crumbling into a pitted parking lot. Old trees shade most of the rest of the street, half hiding low houses and an abandoned gas station. A single car sits in front of the apartments, tires gone, the windows smashed out. There are three units on the ground floor, a set of stairs with a rickety railing, then three more doors upstairs. The apartment door nearest me stands open. An old woman sits just inside on an up-turned milk crate. Her flowery skirt hangs low between her splayed knees. She is singing; when our eyes meet, she stops, stares me down.

"Wait down here with the cases." Mummy touches my shoulder. "Look like some hoodlum waiting to lift the buttons right off your shirt." She carries Paul up the steps and to the first door on the second floor. They disappear inside. A potcake barks down the road and the first fat drops of rain start to fall, woken up, shaken down. I grab the bag with our pantry goods and start for the stairs. From her doorway, the old woman's eyes follow me. Perhaps her glower will ward off thieves and hoodlums.

"Good afternoon," I say.

She inclines her chin so slightly I could have imagined it. I run up, rain pelting my head and arms, and step into the new place. Mummy is in the middle of the room, Paul's small brown body hunkered into her shoulder. The room looks as if it is tired of us already, the sun-bleached blue sofa too short for even one person to stretch out on, a clunky TV with a bulging screen, a coffee table that looks shaky, a lamp, its yellowed shade askew. A small kitchen in one corner, its fridge humming wearily, a dark-ened hallway.

I hold up the bag. "It started raining."

She nods, turning back to the door, as though she had not noticed the downpour. "Guess we're home."

We make up the bed with the blue sheets from my old room, take turns showering in dribbles of cold water, then lie down on the sagging mattress. Mummy's mouth falls open. Paul whimpers a little, then curls up against her and drifts off, too. I can't sleep; I get up and unpack our shoes, line them up against the far wall, heel-mashed slippers and broad, half-shined Mary Janes beside Mummy's slip-on flats for work. On the other side of the wall, voices start off low, then rise till they drown out Mummy's snore, Paul's thick sleep-breath. Something clunks, smacking hard into the wall. Then again. And again. I pull on my pink hoodie and open our front door. The microwave clock says it's just past nine. I step outside. The rain has stopped and the night is still, but, even out here, I can hear the people beside us. I try plugging my ears, but the sound keeps going and I finally give in and let my hands fall. Down the road, one streetlamp dribbles stained yellow light.

"Least everything's washed clean."

I turn. Mummy steps out in her bare feet. She rubs her arms.

"We out of milk," she says.

"I can get it in the morning."

"I have to feed Paul early so we can head out on time."

I can hear the question waiting just behind her words, and my heart starts to pound. I want to ask her if she can go, better yet if we can put Paul in long pants and a sweater, all go together. Then she shivers slightly. She looks small. Her mouth sags at the corners. I swallow. *It's no different than going in the day*, I tell myself. "Okay."

Mummy leans over, kisses my forehead. "My life-saver. Get some chocolate biscuits too."

∞

The next morning, three buses pass me before Tonique appears in the distance, schoolbag over her shoulder. I wave the fourth bus down as she nears.

"Girl, hurry up." I step up as the doors open.

"Not this one." She pulls me back. The driver, an old man with a smooth bald head and a disappointed face, deepens his scowl and closes the door.

"Why?"

"Tell you later. How's the new place?"

"Far from the store."

"So what?"

"Mummy send me last night. Milk."

"In the night?"

My body remembers the *thumthum* of my heart. I shrug, and push the feeling away.

"You like your room?"

"It's okay."

"Oh, this one, this one." She extends a slim arm and waves it delicately. The bus eases over.

"This better have a pool and a mini-bar inside," I say as I climb on. The windows are tinted, the seats plastic-covered and slightly sticky. Nothing special, far as I can see. Tonique sits near the front, beckons me forward. "So? What's so special about this bus?"

"Shhh!" She pulls me down beside her. "Tell you later." Before I can ask more, the music on the bus swings high. Someone cheers. The bus swerves left, throwing me up against Tonique.

"Super Value sellin' bus license now, ay?" a man shouts from the back, and there is laughter, and, for a second, everything is just right.

∞

Our fourth night, I'm nearly asleep on the sofa when Mummy touches my leg, soft. I sit up, feel something crumple under my hand.

"What happen?"

"You mashin' up your homework."

"You wake me up to tell me that?"

"I need you to make a run to the store."

"We outta milk? It was almost full this morning."

Mummy looks over toward the kitchen. "Fridge broken."

"I unpacked some milk in the can."

"It's too heavy, Paul won't drink it."

I stand up fast. "I have to pee."

On my way back from the bathroom, I glance at Paul asleep on the bed. His small body is stretched out free, sprawling across the quilt. His fingers twitch, then relax, his curled hands a pair of small bowls.

"Nicole?" Mummy's voice carries over to me. "Five dollars on the nightstand."

I bite my lip and grab the money. Outside, it is humid and still. At the bottom of the stairs, I pause a second. Singing spills out of the old lady's window.

"'Trust and obey, for there's no other way . . .'" She sings it the way Daddy did, slow, the words stretched tight and thin. Without thinking, I walk toward the music. I sing back to him.

"'Than to trust and obey.'"

She looks up at me through her dark red sheers. "Mmm hmm."

"Evening." I head toward the street. Her song follows me till it can't anymore, and then I carry on under my breath, the music keeping me company, as if Daddy is beside me, humming my insides warm.

"Pssst!"

Across the street. The guy leans against a dusty green car, his face shadowed.

"Good night," I say, looking straight ahead. I try to seem sure of where I'm going—choir practice, to pick up my daughter from youth group. Like I have a full bust that requires a thick-strapped bra. Like I'm not worth bothering with. The owner of the voice lets me pass. I stay close to the edge of the road, hope the shadows cover me.

In the store, I grab the milk and pay. The clock above the door says it's coming up nine. On the way back, I walk fast, too fast for a mother, but the green car has moved on and I am alone on the road.

∞

"You never told me what's with the bus." I squint against the morning sun. Tonique leans against the bus-stop sign.

"Why you sound mad?"

"Tired."

"Gone for milk again?"

"Fridge still ain' fix."

"Oh." She perks up. "See our bus here." It slows and pulls over. She starts up onto the bus and a short, wide woman barrels down into her.

"Let people off first!" the woman snaps. Tonique steps aside, her smile untarnished, then boards when the door is clear. The bus is almost empty today.

"Morning!" She flashes the driver a smile.

"Come here, let me talk to you." The driver grabs her wrist. His face is full of mischief, which makes it seem young. Then his grin expands, and crinkles show at the edges of his eyes. My heart skips and I move forward, shadowing my friend, not sure what I am about to do. But she is still smiling. She squeals and something in my belly twists. I look away and reach past her to drop my coins into the jar. The driver pulls her nearer, whispers something. Tonique yanks her hand away.

"Lend me seventy-five cents," she says to me. Her smile is gone, her eyes down. I count out the fare and drop it into the jar. The coins land in a shower of dull clinks.

"Maybe your friend want to ride for free." The driver looks back at her in the rear-view mirror, his voice an oil slick in a dirty puddle. We sit as far back as we can. I open my mouth and she shakes her head, turns away.

∞

"How old you is?"

The voice accosts me as I am sliding the key into the lock. I look back and into the face of the woman who must be our next-door neighbour. She holds a broom in one hand, a washed-out orange rug in the other. Her voice sounds lower than it did through the wall, and her eyes are hard, as though we've spoken before and it did not go well.

"Pardon me?"

"I see you laughin' up with that driver. How old you is?"

"Fifteen." After I answer, I wonder why I owed her this word.

"Fifteen." She spits it back out at me like it's raw dough. "Your ma know you carry on like that?"

I push the door open.

"Don't you bring no nastiness in this building, you understand?"

I slam the door shut, then roll the windows closed. Flecks and grit hit the flattened panes while the woman beats out her dirt for me to breathe in.

∞

That night, after we've eaten, Mummy shoves the takeout containers back in the fridge and turns the TV up so she can listen while she does the dishes. Her phone rings.

"What? Man, don't think you could disappear all day, then just—hold on." She waves to get my attention. "Do me a favour, take Paul in the tub. I need some fresh air."

I run the bathwater for a minute, till it clears, then strip Paul down and plop him in. As I wash him, I search his round cheeks, his large, gentle eyes, for something of me, some feature we share, but all I can see is his father. When Mummy comes back in, Paul is clean and ready for bed. She drops the phone onto the bureau. Her eyes are red.

"What'd *he* want?"

"Nothing." She sits down on the bed beside us. "I need you go to the store for me."

"Again? Why I gotta go every night?"

She fumbles in her purse. "Get a pack of saltine crackers and—"

"Milk? I know." I stare at the bills in her extended hand.

"I don't need no backtalking. Go get the things, please."

"Like we sponsoring a whole cow." I take the money and shove it in my pocket, then cram my feet into my shoes. My heart thuds so hard my ears ring. I can feel the night air before I open the door, in my nose, on my skin. The low voice *Pssst. Pssst.* From deep in the apartment, I hear the shower cut on. I pull the door closed behind me.

The sound hits me halfway down the stairs. It comes from above, from the apartment beside ours. The man first, *uuhh, uuhh, uuhh* like a pig. Then the woman, *oh, oh, oh, oh, oh, oh.* My legs can't move me forward for a long second. Below, the old woman is singing. I want to move toward that, to stand long in her doorway, to join in verse after verse. But my face is hot and my armpits prickle. The people beside us shift their pitch louder. I bite my lip and force myself down the stairs, through the empty parking lot, out of the yard. *Milk*, I tell myself. *Milk and saltines.* But under that all I can hear is *uuhh, uuhh, oh, oh, oh.*

∞

The store is stark. Bleach fumes make my nose sting. I stare at the shelf where the milk should be.

"We out, miss." The stock boy's face appears between the shelves. "Check back tomorrow."

I weave through the aisles to the crackers, then loop around. Maybe if I take long, when I get home, it will be quiet. I pause in the baking aisle. Flour, sugar. Then my eye lands on an unfamiliar package. Dry milk. I pick up a box and study the directions. *Mix 1/3 cup powdered milk into a cup of water, or add to baked goods for added richness. Store in a cool, dry place. Refrigerate milk once rehydrated.* I grab a second box, then a third.

∞

As I turn onto our street, it starts sprying, a fine mist that barely wets the ground. Jasmine blooms somewhere. Its scent curls around my nose, over my shoulder, loops my waist. I step into our yard. Through her sheers, the old woman sings, *What a friend we have in Jesus,* but the air is so dense only every few words reach me. A car is parked near the old woman's apartment. Grey and shiny. *I know this car,* I think, and *she wouldn't,* and *she did.*

I take the stairs in doubles, triples, running the last few steps to our door. I let myself in. I don't even need to look to know there will be a pair of men's loafers by the door. Through the walls there is the rumble of muffled conversation, a hair dryer's hum. I walk to the fridge and yank its door open. Stale air belches out at me. In the dark, I can make out a nearly full bottle of milk. I open it and its scent rises, animal, tart. I pour it down the sink and start down the hall. The voices stop my feet before I reach the bedroom door.

"Already?" Paul's daddy's voice is low. "I just got here."

"Been an hour." Mummy. "She soon reach back. Go."

I stumble back down the hallway. The room stinks of sour milk. The fridge door still hangs open, calling me. I step toward its silent body. Something makes me peer behind it. The cord snakes onto the floor, a spent tongue. The prongs glint like silver teeth. I bend down, rub a finger over the cold metal, then push it back into the socket. The fridge bursts into life, a weary hum filling the air.

My head swirls with a thousand sounds, *uh uh*, *oh*, *pssst*, *the glory, tomorrow great things* and above them all, the refrigerator's low, mocking whir. I can't think—I need to be somewhere, anywhere, that isn't this cramped place. I whirl around toward the door—the grocery bag catches my eye and I grab it, though I don't know where I plan to go, what I should do. The front door springs open under my hand. I step out. Larger drops are falling now. I pull the door closed behind me. I take two steps before the grey plastic bag tears, spilling boxes of milk powder onto the walkway.

There is a moment, or five, where everything seems perfectly still. The old woman's song is silent, no car passes through, and I can't seem to move. There is only the heavy, steady rain, and the puddles that bloom around my feet, around the ripped bag. I bend down. Maybe I can salvage it.

"What happen to you, girl, you crazy? What you doin' in this weather? Sneakin' out?"

I turn and look up. The neighbour stands behind me, her thin nightdress near see-through. I turn back to the mangled mess.

"You hear me? Don't bring no trouble round here!"

The rain has pooled in the bag. As I lift it, white liquid trickles out and over my feet, pale and weak.

Through the mist, her voice burns like hot water on skin. "Too damn fresh."

LAUNDRY

TWO MINUTES OF PEACE. Two minutes of peace, and now this boy won't leave me.

"What? What, TJ, what? No, you can't go by Grammy. Go inside, watch your cartoons. Go."

Tch. Can't have a moment to myself. Laundry never done. Work never done. Two more loads I need to do before they cut the lights off. How I supposed to pay this, now? And then Travis school fee. Wow. Thank God for two minutes alone. Anyway, all things sort out somehow. Like Grammy used to say. Maybe Mrs. Gardiner need some help.

"TJ, get back in that damn house, man, how much times I have to tell you?"

Oh, this piece a breeze feel good. Tch. Let me go over there, see if Mrs. Gardiner home.

"Mrs. Gardiner! Mrs. Gardiner!"

"Hey!"

Look at her. You can almost see the money drip off her. Just get her hair do. When last I had couple extra dollars to say do my hair?

"I have a question for you."

"Yeah, Debra. What happen, you alright?"

"Mmm hmm, right here. You need any help with your wash?"

"How your mummy?"

Oh, here we go. Gotta go through all kinda long talks, how this one, how that one, how much food in ya fridge, what Travis daddy doing for you.

"She's fine."

"Pressure still high?"

"Well, you know she take medication."

"I saw something on the computer the other day, this special herb they say all but cure pressure."

Nod, *mm hmm*, nod. Gotta play like I care. She know just what I come over here for, why she have to make me almost beg for it?

"I'll have to see if I can find that information."

"Yeah, or I could print it off, you take it to her. You have a printer?"

She know my internet off, why she think the only TV she can hear now is ZNS?

"Not right now."

"Anyway, what you come to ask me?"

"If you need any help with your laundry."

"Laundry?" Mrs. Gardiner's face mashes up in confusion, like I didn't do two loads of baby clothes for her grandkids last week, like I didn't do all her linens week before that.

"Yeah, I know you have your grands over here sometimes, I just thought with the extra people in the house . . ."

Don't lean too hard.

"Not this week, Debbie. My oldest up by her next grammy, and the other two gone by they daddy."

"Oh, okay." What's that rustling in the grass, now? If those people over there don't keep their dog from round me . . . "Oh, TJ, that's you." When did he get so tall? Head almost up to my waist. Even though his arms can't quite reach to touch when he hugs me. That's about my size, not his. "Yes, baby, Mummy have big legs. Grunting and stretching ain' ga change that, your arms just have to grow."

"Travis, you bein' a good boy?"

TJ mashes his face against my side. That's right, don't look at that old she-devil. "Playin' shy, now. Did you say 'good afternoon'?"

His head is a small sphere under my palm. "I guess he don't feel like talking today." If I break out in a smile right now . . . "I don't know what to do with him."

"You gotta be firm with him, that's what."

She don't want me remind her how that same oldest granddaughter got kicked out of dance class for squeezing half a bottle of glitter glue in another girl's ballet shoes. "Go on, TJ. Go inside the house, since you don't want talk." No, don't hang around here whining; you should be thanking me. Don't linger in the doorway for all the neighbourhood flies to come in! Tch. "Close the door, please!"

"What his daddy doin' for him these days?"

Here we go. She want me roll out my pity parade. "He'll send a something here and there when he can."

Mrs. Gardiner sucks her teeth. "*When he can?* What is *when he can?* When you have a child you gotta do every day. Travis don't eat when he can, he gotta eat every day. Right?"

Matter of fact, I have him on a strict eating schedule. Every other Tuesday, and if he's good, twice on Saturday and Sunday. "Yeah, that's true."

"That's why I's give thanks for Mr. Gardiner every day. We been married thirty-two years. That's something, eh?"

Thirty-two years of that big-belly, stale-breath man climbing on top of you? That long, saggy face hanging down over top of your prissy expression? What a sight that must be. Child, you can have that. Bet you he's still try too.

"Ah, that's better. I like to see you smile, I's hate for people to be sad and broken-down. Let me check the hamper. I think I do have couple things you could wash for me."

∞

"Mummy, how come we get to use the candle tonight?" TJ's skin looks so smooth in this light. He seems smaller too.

"I already tell you. You know why we's use the candle."

"Why, Mummy?"

"Because we need to save money and candles are cheaper."

"Oh."

"We could pretend we in a big storm, all the lights off, the wind howling outside."

There's that wide smile, his moonlight-white teeth.

"I like the candles better. I wish we couldn't pay for the light bill every night."

You might be in luck, baby boy. "Make sure behind your ears clean by the time I come back."

"Where you goin', Mummy?"

"Nowhere." Who told this room to shrink? I need air and this window can't open any more. "I just left something outside." Bright lights on at Mrs. Gardiner's—must be nice. Only noise from my house the spinning, spinning, spinning of the machine. There's the new neighbour across the way, weedy little man, going out to his car. "Alright, good night!" Why he always gotta be coming or going? He can't stay one place? And, there's the spin cycle, banging around like rutting elephants loose in the pots and pans. I know I ga find the sheets all on one side of the washing machine. Off-balance, like my life.

"Excuse me."

Here we go. Miss Thing from the other side of the

duplex. What she name again? "Hey, how are you tonight?"

"You plan on washing much longer? My baby trying to sleep."

What the hell you think mine doing? "Oh, sorry." Now Mr. Dandelion's out of his car, perched up on the hood like some forgotten pinup girl. "Shouldn't be too long."

"My husband just put him down. He's a light sleeper, you know?"

Now he want wave? I already said goodnight, how many more times do we have to say hello?

"Hi, Ricky!"

So the baby can't doze through a wash cycle but her megaphone lungs don't bother his sleep.

She turns back to me. "You think another half hour or . . . ?"

Miss, if you take that plastic wig off, you won't have to scratch your head so much. "Something like that." Give or take a couple hours. That's right, go back inside to your a/c. You can bang your door closed all you like. "Don't wake your baby, now!" Like sifting through Mrs. Gardiner's stale towels is a spa day for me. Forty dollars. Just let me get that forty dollars.

∞

I'm sure I slept. So why do I feel like I've been washing all night and hanging up these clean things from before sun-up? First sheets, then towels, next underclothes. Oops—can't drop Mrs. Gardiner's delicates. Might miss and bring her down to earth. "TJ, come out from under those sheets!" I don't have time for jokes, I gotta finish this.

"Look, Mummy." Look at his face, bright with mischief. Almost think he's glowing with dew. "We could use these as a shower curtain!"

"If you don't put that woman panties down, boy." Whoo. Let me catch my breath, if she hear me laughing out here she ga think I don't need money. "Get your things together for school, please."

"You should see how Miss Demeritte does when someone come in late, Mummy." Morning light on his face picks up the baby fuzz on his skin. My gold.

"How she do? Show me."

Little bottom out, finger waggling, head wiggling, feet stamping the grass down. Oh, I can't laugh and I can't help it.

"Um, hey, good morning."

Ah, here we go. That same one across the street. Why he over by our garbage cans like a hungry dog? "Hello."

Let me just keep reaching in the basket for laundry. Ugh, more of Mrs. Gardiner's infernal panties. At least they may chase him away. Don't smirk. Don't smirk. "You need something?"

"It's, uh. Well, I saw your lawn was a little high. Um, can I cut your grass for you?"

"You have a problem with the grass?"

"No, your grass is very—I don't mean—I just have—"

"You have what?"

"I have . . . uh . . . just that I have a lawnmower, and I'm off work today, you see—"

"I don't have money for no lawn cutting." Too early for all this beating about the bush.

"I wasn't going to charge. Just a favour."

So I look like I was born yesterday. "No thanks."

"No obligation. Just helping a neighbour out."

"My grandmother always used to say, nothing in this life for free."

"I didn't mean nothing bad by it, Miss."

"Boy, get down out the guava tree and go inside, put your socks and shoes on." This man still here? He must not have a hobby.

"So, I can cut the lawn for you?"

"Sure, if that's what you want. Go ahead."

∞

"Mummy!" Travis drops my hand. "What happen to the yard?"

Hmph. So he actually did it. "Someone cut it for us, baby."

"The dead branch is off the guava tree, too."

"Hey, Debra!"

Mrs. Gardiner's sense of smell could put a bloodhound to shame.

"You got my wash ready?"

"Yes, ma'am." Let me get it over with and get my cash. "Don't go in the road, TJ." I can do this in one trip, just stack it up high, and walk slow. It isn't heavy. It's a basket of bubbles. It's cotton balls wrapped up in fluff. "Alright, Mrs. Gardiner. Clean, folded, and ready to go."

"Your friend been over here today."

"I bleached the whites extra for you so they should be extra fresh." She have to rub up the towels like that? They hard, ma'am. You want 'em soft, buy Egyptian cotton. Only so much I could do with discount terry.

"That little bony one across the road. Ricky."

"And I pressed the sheets for you, like you asked." Can we expedite to the part where I get my money?

"No, no, no, don't put the bed linens on the dining table. People *sleep* on those things."

Forty dollars. Keep it cool. Forty dollars. "My mistake. Let me set them down on the chair."

"Smell different. What type detergent you used?"

"Tide."

"No, no, I don't use that kind. Next time you need to get the fragrance-free one, my grandbaby has allergies, I thought I told you that. I saw him coming over this morning with his yard tools. He always out there, looking you up and down. And you know they only want one thing."

"May want to hang up these blouses so they don't crease."

"You better watch out for him."

She's onto the t-shirts, now. What did I even bother with them for, if she was ga undo my work and fold it up her way? Next time I might as well dump a pile of things on her doorstep and let her do it herself.

"You gotta do it this way so you don't get that crease in the front. You know we like to look fresh. Mr. Gardiner especially. He have high standards."

Choice of spouse to the contrary. "I understand."

"Alright, then. Like I say, you look out for that man, you know how they's go, dip in, dip out, and leave you right there with the baby. Thank God Mr. Gardiner was never like that, but most of these men round here . . . Well, you know."

Finally, she paying me. "Thank you." I can't stand when people roll the money up like a cigar. Surprised she didn't iron the bills out too. Maybe rolled is good enough for the likes of me. Hold on, now—a twenty, five ones. This a joke? "Mrs. Gardiner, I thought we agreed on forty."

"Yeah, but remember I over-paid you last time?"

Over-what? I didn't sleep till after eleven, up at five, and—my light bill. No.

"I might have some more stuff for you later on, though, if you want to work for the rest. You ga be home?"

I need to get out of here. If I stay in here . . .

"Nope."

"I'll leave it outside your door, then. Another three loads, you could do that for me for fifteen, right? That'll bring us up to forty."

I should tell her about stealing, about not paying a mother with a child on her own, about that big wad of money she's shoving back in her purse, to spend on what? More hard towels? More big old ugly panties? Once that next notice come, my lights getting cut off . . . "Yes, Mrs. Gardiner." If I grit my teeth any harder they may break off in my mouth. "No problem." I shouldn't slam the door on my way out.

Who's that snickering? Wonderful, now Plastic Wig laughing at me.

"Rough day?"

Let me breathe. Let me just walk across into my yard and breathe.

"Mummy, wanna see me cartwheel?"

"Hold on, TJ." I can't think about it. I can't. Let me just look at what's around me. Bare clothesline that gets more rest than me. Crooked lines on raggedy-short grass. That man must have dragged the mower across the lawn with his backside. If I close my eyes, it may look better. All of this.

"Mummy, watch this!"

"Not now, TJ. Inside."

"But Mummy—"

I'm the reason his voice is so small.

"Come in and get your homework finished while we have daylight."

"Five more minutes!"

File through the mail again. Visa, junk mail, religious pamphlet. "Now, Travis." Here it is. Island Electrics. Let me sit down. Of course the envelope won't tear open properly. Where did I put the opener?

"You don't even wanna see what I can do?"

"Get inside!" What sense does it even make to open up this letter? I know what it says. And I don't have the money. Whoever that is with those big-people footsteps, just go. Now is not the time.

"Go ahead, baby, let me see you!"

"Mrs. Gardiner? You wanna see me cartwheel?"

No. Absolutely not, I'm dreaming. She can't be out here watching TJ, after she—and I know she heard me call him.

"Show Mr. Gardiner, show Mr. Gardiner! Way to go, TJ! Oh, you so strong!"

What sense would it even make for me to call him again now? He sounds happy, sounds like seven should.

∞

Oh, my neck. Who tell me sleep out on the sofa all night? The house all flooded with light . . . When you're too tired to even close the curtains the night before.

"Get up, TJ. Hurry up, go bathe off. We need to leave."

There's the clothes basket out on the doorstep, must have been there for hours. If Mrs. Gardiner sees that, I can kiss that last fifteen dollars goodbye. Wait—empty? Where they gone?

"Mummy, you washed last night?"

A line, a long line of clean clothes, lifting in the wind—how? "No, I just got up, same as you."

Movement across the road. That man don't rest, hey? Out here already, mowing his lawn again. Oh, there he goes, I don't need to hear to know he said *Good morning*.

"No, baby. It was a miracle."

∞

Ten dollars. Ten dollars. Short me by five. Who's the bigger fool here, her for being so wicked, or me for letting her do it?

"So, I can drop another load over tonight?"

Oh, she think she slick, with that sly smile. Watch who's gonna be the fool this time. "Yes."

∞

"Mummy, what we come to the mall for."

"Don't worry about it, TJ. Pick up your feet please."

"Why we goin' in the bookstore? Can I get a book?"

"Go look in the kids' section." Oh, there's Laura from school. "Hey, girl."

"Hey, Debbie. Long time. You got big since I last saw you, what happen?"

"See him over there by the comics?"

"Oh, I know, I couldn't drop that last ten pounds after I had my second one."

And it all went in your head, apparently. "Listen, do me a favour. I have to pick something up and I can't take him with me, you understand?"

"You got a date? My shift over in an hour—"

"No, I won't be that long. I just need to go in one store."

"Go ahead, I'll watch him."

∞

Morrison's is closest, but their panties and bras all look too cheap. Let me cut across to La Femme Nuit. Look at these bras and little stringy nighties. Aha! Satiny and red. Extra-small. This ridiculous lacy concoction couldn't even fit half my left forearm. Perfect.

Let me hurry up get back to the bookstore. Ah, here we go, TJ safe, sound, and eyebrow deep in the comic section. Hold on, that man at the counter look familiar. Wait—this man following me or what?

"So, uh—if you change your mind and decide you're hiring, just—uh, keep me in mind. Please."

Don't look this way. Don't look this way, last thing I need is more awkward—

"Mummy! Guess what, Miss Laura said I could have this book for half price, and look, see our neighbour from across the street? Why you crouched down like that, you hiding?"

"Hush." So much for saving dignity. "Afternoon, Ricky. How are you?"

"Ah, you know. Just, uh, dropping off my resumé. I should, uh—make a few more stops."

"Mummy, how come—"

"Hush."

"But Mummy, the bottom of his shoes almost gone."

How did I never notice how worn Ricky's shoes are?

"And he came to ask for a job looking like that? Why, Mummy?"

"Because, Travis." People do what they have to.

∞

Oh, this wash must be made of diamonds, I feel so rich. I don't even care if we have beans from a can every night for a month.

"Mummy, you humming. You happy?"

"Sure am, TJ."

"Oh. What's this?"

My child holding wet laundry over the floor and I don't even feel a glimmer of vexation. "You making a puddle, TJ."

"Looks like the doily Aunt Mavis keeps on her side tables."

"Never mind." Well, look at that. I can feel the hum building up in my chest again already. "Put it back in the sink. That one's important, baby."

∞

I don't care if I get Travis to school five minutes late. Wash done and on the line, but I can't leave without doing this one last thing. Let me knock a second time. Must be sleeping.

"Yeah? You see what time it is?"

"It's your neighbour!"

"Oh! Ah, morning." Poor man didn't even wipe the sleep out of his eye.

"Sorry, guess I woke you. I just cooked too much this morning, and our fridge—anyway, we don't have space for extra food. I brought you some. It's tuna and grits." Let me push it in his hands and go. Last thing I need is awkward all over again.

∞

"So, we agreed on what for the laundry this time, Deb? Eight?"

"That's fine. Times hard."

"I know. I feel for you, being a single mother and all. That's why—"

"I mean for you. I don't mind giving you a break this time. Things tough, right?"

"No, no, no, no. No, you wait right there."

Here she goes, disappearing into her back room. Digging around for her purse. Better get that money.

"It ain't a matter of affording." Bills in her hand. Good. "I thought we was neighbours. We right next to each other. I thought we could help each other out."

"Of course." Let me plaster on my sweet smile. A five, and three bills. "Oh, thank you *so* much. I'm glad to help you out. You want to check the laundry over this time?"

"No, no, that's alright."

"Okay, then." Hurry up come out this woman house. This yard too big, let me run. I can't be too close. Duck down behind the clothesline, though. I want hear every word. One, two, three, four, and—

"Gardiner! Ivan Gardiner, what is this? What is this? What is this blasphemy I find in my laundry?"

"Mummy, what we playing?" Like he knows something's afoot. "How come Mrs. Gardiner sound mad?"

"Hush, boy. We listening."

"Honey—I swear, I never seen nothing like that. Extra-small, that isn't your size. Where that come from?"

"That's what I want to know. Who own it is, Ivan? Where it come from? Tell me now! Where?"

I can barely straighten up. I gotta hold the laughter in and I can't, I about to burst. I gotta get inside. Hurry up open this door. Ah, Ricky sitting on his front lawn, watching, waving.

"Can I come over, Miss? I want ask you something."

Nod, best I can. Nearly there, through the door, my shoulders are heaving, my chest and middle and everything. I can't hold it much longer. Here it comes.

"I knew it, Ivan! I knew you was stepping out on me!"

Oh, my sides . . . oh, my face hurts—I can't hear, I should hush and I can't hush this laughter. Where's the light switch? Flick it on and—nothing. Let me lean on the wall, catch myself. No, I can't—be caught. I open my mouth all the way and let my head go back. Laughter lifts out of me. Is that TJ's voice mirroring mine? There is so much joy he must be laughing too. Can't see anything, eyes full of tears, squeeze them shut and still that sound rises. The room is all lit up with orange. Let it come. Let it find every dark corner of my home.

ACKNOWLEDGEMENTS

Thank you to my wonderful editor, Melanie Tutino, whose understanding, vision and keen eye guided this collection to its final form.

I am entirely grateful for my agent and friend Rachel Letofsky for helping these stories find light and home.

To the design team—the visuals are a dream.

Eternal love to my small family. Jason, you helped me to safeguard my writing space. Nyssa, you shared me when you could, encouraged me to save frequently, and diligently inserted the letter N in each draft. Kayari, you stretched my heart and bent time.

Last, to my people, the people of The Bahamas, my lilt and lyric, my earth, my blood.

JANICE LYNN MATHER is the author of two acclaimed novels for young adults: *Learning to Breathe*, which was a finalist for the Governor General's Literary Award, and *Facing the Sun*, which won the Amy Mathers Teen Book Award. She lives in Vancouver. *Uncertain Kin* is her adult debut.

Uncertain Kin is set in Adobe Caslon, a digitized typeface based on the original 1734 designs of William Caslon. Caslon is generally regarded as the first British typefounder of consequence and his fonts are considered, then as now, to be among the world's most "user-friendly" text faces.

01 14

1 J